THE SILENCER

THE SIGNAL

THE SILENCER

THE SILENCER SERIES BOOK 1

MIKE RYAN

WWW.MIKERYANBOOKS.COM

1

London—Nobody could remember exactly when or how long the unidentified man had been waiting in the hospital lobby. It was a busy night, and he never checked in at the desk or asked for assistance. It wasn't until he fell off the chair and laid unconscious on the floor that anybody really paid much attention to him. His long trench coat had covered up the gunshot wound to his stomach, but his white shirt had now turned red thanks to blood soaking into it for a few hours. They immediately took him to the emergency room and put him on the operating table. The doctors needed to take the bullet out and stop the bleeding as soon as possible. After an hour of surgery, the doctors successfully removed the bullet. Luckily for the man, no major organs had been damaged, other than a very minor graze to part of his liver. Once he was stitched up, they wheeled him to the fifth floor and a private room for his recovery.

MIKE RYAN

A couple of hours after the surgery, the man had awoken in a considerable amount of pain. He was holding his side and feeling where the bandages now were. He grimaced as he looked around at his surroundings, not remembering how he got there. A few minutes later a nurse came in to check on him.

"Hey!" The smiling nurse greeted him. "Nice to finally see you awake."

"Hi."

"How are you feeling?"

"I've had better days."

"Yeah, I bet. My name's Kelly. Can I get you anything?"

"Yeah. My release papers."

She laughed. "That might take a little while."

"I can't stay here," he said.

"Why? You in some sort of trouble? Is that what the gunshot was from? Somebody after you? I can get the police here for you."

"No. Don't call the police."

Kelly looked at him a little strangely. The police would be there anyway, but usually the people that came in there that didn't want the police involved were in most cases running from them. Not that it mattered to her in how she treated the patient. Law-breaking or law-abiding, she did her duties the same way no matter what.

"You didn't have any identification on you when you came in," Kelly said. "What's your name?"

The man thought about it for a minute, knowing what would happen if he revealed his true name. At least the

2

one he was going by now. If he gave that, his name would ping up in somebody's computer and they could come back to try to finish the job.

"Uh... it's John. John Smith."

Kelly raised her eyebrows as she looked at him over the top of the clipboard that she was writing on. She knew it was a fake name right away, but being an experienced nurse of over ten years, knew not to take issue with it. If that was the name he wanted to use, that was his business.

"John Smith, huh? That's what you're gonna go with?" She scribbled on his notes then hung the clipboard over the end of his bed.

"Yeah."

"You remember how you got here?"

"Umm... no, not really."

"Apparently, you were waiting in the lobby and you suddenly passed out. Nobody could remember when you came in or if somebody brought you in."

"I came in on my own."

"So, you remember. Anybody you want me to call to let them know you're here?" She knew what his answer would be.

"No."

"Friends, family, anyone?"

"I don't have any friends or family here."

Kelly stayed with him for a few more minutes, asking him some more questions that he mostly evaded. She checked his vital signs, all of which seemed to be OK. As she wrapped things up, she let Smith know that a doctor would be in to see him in a few minutes. That doctor wound up walking in about ten minutes later.

"Mr..." The doctor picked up the chart and examined it, "Smith. I'm Dr. Karlson. How are you feeling?"

"Fantastic."

"Well, considering what happened, I'd say you're a very lucky man. We removed the bullet. Luckily it didn't hit any major organs... well, it did hit a very tiny piece of your liver, but it was such a small piece it really wasn't much at all. Most people with a gunshot to their stomach or abdomen don't fare quite as well as you."

"No kidding. So, what's my recovery timeline?" Smith said.

"You should be up and about and out of here in two or three days I'd say."

"Long-term effects?"

"Difficult to say right now. Full recovery will be anywhere from three to six months if you don't do anything too strenuous. No climbing mountains or obstacle courses or anything like that. You never truly know whether someone will ever get back to a hundred percent after something like this. Some people will get to eighty or ninety percent and that's as far as they'll ever go. Now, you seem like you're in decent shape so I would imagine you'll get there, if not, then pretty close to it."

After Smith's conversation with the doctor, he worried about what might happen next. He knew that the law required the hospital to notify the police of a gunshot injury. Since gunshot wounds were not very common in

England, Smith knew the police would be there soon, and with questions he didn't want to answer.

He hit the button for the nurse's station to get Kelly. She came in just a few seconds.

She poked her head around the door. "What can I do for you?"

"Is there any way I can get a shirt or something? Kind of cold just laying here like this."

"I should be able to find something. Give me a couple of minutes."

"Thank you." Smith smiled.

He was going to have to speed up his recovery time and exit the hospital sooner than the doctors had planned. He couldn't risk the police asking questions and poking around. It only took five minutes for Kelly to return with a plain black shirt.

"This OK?" She held it up for him as she walked in.

"Should do fine. Thank you."

"Got you a large. You don't quite look like a medium."

"Just my size," Smith said, slowly putting the shirt on. "Better?"

"Yes. Any idea on when the police will be here?"

"The police?"

"Yeah. They're coming, right? Gunshot wounds have to be reported, right?"

A little taken aback by the questions, Kelly wondered why he was inquiring. It seemed strange to her. "I believe they were just called. Thirty minutes ago? Everything OK?"

"Everything's fine. Just wanted to know when to expect company. Could you just give me a minute or two's notice when they get here? I hate surprises."

"Sure thing."

It took a few minutes for him to come up with a plan, but Smith knew anything was better than staying there. He unhooked all his monitors and gingerly got off the bed, walking over to the window where his trench coat was draped over a chair. Just as he was putting it on, Kelly came rushing into the room.

"What do you think you're doing?" She stood in front of him, hands on hips.

"I'm afraid I have to go."

"Oh, no you don't. You're gonna lay right back down," she said, gripping his arm.

Smith resisted and gently removed her hand from his bicep. "Thank you for patching me up and everything but staying here isn't an option."

Kelly objected again, but he shrugged off her attempts to keep him there. Smith walked out of the room and down the hall, right past a team of doctors and nurses, all of whom were wondering what was going on.

"You still need attention." Kelly stayed two steps behind him.

"You've done enough," Smith said, not even bothering to turn around.

He kept walking until he found an elevator, Kelly running after him. Once the doors opened, he stepped in and pushed for the main floor, Kelly just barely getting in before the doors closed again.

"What do you think you're doing?" Kelly said, watching the brightly lit numbers count down.

"Leaving."

"Can I ask why?"

"Already told you. Can't stay here."

"Who are you running from?"

"You don't wanna know."

"The police? Or a criminal?"

"Neither."

"What else is there?"

"There are people looking for me more powerful than either of those. And once they know I'm here, they'll come looking for me," Smith said.

"We can try to protect you while you heal."

"Afraid not. Not from these people."

"How do you know?"

"Because I used to be one of them."

"Used to be?"

"Up until last night."

The elevator doors opened and Smith walked out, Kelly following for a few steps. Eventually she stopped without saying another word, knowing that there was nothing else she could do to prevent him from leaving. A couple of police officers entered the hospital and walked right past Smith on his way to the exit. As soon as he passed the officers, Smith looked back at Kelly, wondering if she'd inform them of his presence. Kelly looked at the officers but let them pass by her without a word, watching them get into the elevator. Smith looked at the nurse and gave a smile, nodding slightly as if to say thank you to her.

"Take care of yourself," she said.

Philadelphia—It'd been six months since his shooting and he figured he'd spent enough time laying low. After arriving at Philadelphia International Airport, Smith had just picked up his bags and started walking through the corridor when he stopped suddenly. There was a man standing there, holding a placard with his name on it. John Smith. There was a second man standing next to the one with the sign.

He sighed, resigned to the fact that they had finally found him, ready to submit to what had started in London. He knew it would be futile to resist, knowing that agents were watching from several locations. He took a quick glance around to see if he could spot any guns with him in its sights, though he couldn't pick anyone out. The man put his hand out, indicating to Smith that he should follow him.

Ready to accept whatever was coming, he followed the man over to a restaurant. Smith was instructed to wait there while the man walked over to a table where another gentleman was sitting. Sitting with his back to him, and dressed in a nice black suit, Smith couldn't make out the identity of the person. From behind, it didn't appear to be anyone that he'd ever met before. The man waved Smith over to have a seat with the gentleman that was sitting, who never turned around to look at him. Smith walked leisurely over to the table, not keen to hear whatever the person had to say to him. Smith sat down across from the well-dressed man, still unsure who the hell he was. He wasn't the type of person Smith expected to see if he was ever caught. The man was eating tomato soup but stopped when Smith sat.

"Mr. Smith, it's a pleasure to meet you," the man said, putting his hand out.

Smith wasn't sure about shaking hands, but decided to do so, anyway. "Wish I could say the same to you but you seem to have the advantage of actually knowing who I am. I can't say the same about you."

"You can call me David," the man said in a quiet, unassuming voice.

"Got a last name?"

"Just David will do for now."

"How'd you know my name?"

"Which one?"

"Either."

"I have ways. Though I would think a man such as yourself would be able to come up with a better alias than Smith."

"I was in a hurry. You work for Centurion?" Smith said.

"You can put your mind at ease, Mr. Smith. I can assure you I'm not with the CIA, or any other government agency for that matter. I'm not here to harm you in any way."

"Then how do you know who I am? How'd you know I would be here?"

"There are many things that I'm aware of that I probably shouldn't be. That's something we can discuss at another time."

"What do you want from me?" Smith shifted slightly on the hard, plastic seat.

"Well since you seem to be in transition at the moment with regards to your work, I wanted to offer you employment."

"Doing what?"

"Similar to your last line of work," David said. "Only hopefully without all the killing."

"Listen, I'm not sure what this is all about but you seem to talk without really telling me anything. Why don't you just tell me what you really want?"

David opened his mouth to start talking, but hesitated as he tried to formulate what he wanted to say. "My... goal, my aim, what I hope to accomplish... is to prevent bad things happening to good people. To do that, I need someone I can trust; who has your particular set of skills."

"Bad things happen to good people all the time. You can't prevent it."

"But you can. I can. And if you choose to help me in this pursuit... then we can."

"What're you, a detective or something?"

David grimaced, "Not quite."

"Well then I'm not quite interested," Smith said, standing up. "Am I free to go?" He looked at the two men sitting a few tables away.

"If you like," David nodded. "But I think it's safe to say that if I could find you, I'm pretty sure Centurion would be able to as well."

"Let me worry about that."

"What you need is a friend who can help you in that regard."

"I'm all out of friends. Besides, you look like you should be working in a library or something. I doubt you can help me against Centurion."

"Looks can be deceiving, Mr. Smith. For instance, it's a good thing you left the hospital in London when you did. Not only did you manage to just barely avoid the police, but Centurion agents came about two hours later to check on the man with a gunshot wound to his stomach who had no ID on him."

Smith sat again, wondering how he knew all that. "How'd you get that information if you don't work for Centurion? You're not British, so you're not MI6 either."

"Let's just say I'm good with computers and finding information that others can't."

"Which means you're either a hacker that's on some type of government radar or you've worked for one of the agencies before. So, which is it?"

"A little bit of both I would say," David picked up his spoon. "I'd also like to let you know that it's a good thing you had this unscheduled layover here. There were several agents waiting for you at your original destination down in Orlando. I'm quite sure they would not be giving you the courtesy of this conversation that we're having." He dipped his spoon in his bowl and slurped a mouthful of soup.

Intrigued, Smith was now interested in finding out more, though he was still suspicious. Six years in the CIA had that effect on people. "If you want me to join this crusade that you got going on, then you're going to have to spill a whole lot more information. Like exactly who you are, what you do, and how you get all this information you have. You seem to know everything about me but I know nothing about you. For all I know you're just setting me up for a hit later."

"I assure you, Mr. Smith, that is not the case."

"I'm sure you can understand my suspicions."

"I can. Fine," David said. After a little deliberation, he continued. "I'll tell you a little about myself. How I get my information, well, I should keep that a little more guarded. At least until I know you're as invested in this as I am."

"I'm all ears. You can start by telling me your name."

"My name is David Jones."

"Jones? You gave me crap about Smith and you're using a name like Jones?"

"I'm not supposed to be as creative as you with this alias thing. You should be better at it."

"It is an alias?"

"Yes."

"So, why do you need an alias?"

Jones pushed his bowl of soup aside for a moment as he thought of where to begin. "I, at one point, worked for the NSA. I had the highest level clearance as an analyst and consultant."

"OK?"

"At least, until several months ago. I'd become disillusioned with the agency over the way they process and act on the information that they acquire."

"In what way?"

"As you're well aware, the NSA keeps tabs on everyone.

They have mountains upon mountains of data and information, most of which the public is never aware of. In addition to trying to track terrorist activity, as well as gaining foreign intelligence, they track everything that normal people do. They have access to emails, phone calls, voice messages, almost anything you can think of, they are privy to," Jones said.

"And you take issue with this?"

"Not in its basic context. They're looking for items in reference to national security and I believe in that regard, nothing should be left to chance."

"So, what do you have a problem with, then?"

"That they have access to millions of documents, emails and the rest that they do nothing with. Normal, everyday people, that have real problems, whose lives may be in danger, and the NSA does nothing to help them."

"And if the NSA were to act on that information, or forward it to local authorities, that information couldn't be used in court or else it would be learned where that information came from," Smith said.

Jones nodded his head. "And there'd be a public outcry, more than there already is about the use of the NSA's methods in acquiring such information."

"And how do you propose on helping these so-called normal people?"

"I've devised a program where I have access to some of that information," Jones said, sliding his bowl back in front of him.

"You're hacking the NSA?"

Jones scooped up soup as he considered his answer.

"Uh, well, I guess you could put it that way. I prefer to think of it as piggybacking to get the proper information that I need."

"Do they know this yet?"

"Not that I can tell. It's only a matter of time, however, that they do. But by that time, by the time they've located the source, the signal will be bounced around all over the country. I'm not particularly worried about them finding me. At least not yet. What I'm more concerned with, is acting upon the information that we acquire."

"Just what information is that? What kind of help do these people need? And how are you finding people who need it?" Smith said, eyeing the bowl of soup. He was hungry after his flight and it smelled great.

"The NSA has software programs that scan every email sent, every phone call made, every voice mail, every post on Facebook, every tweet on Twitter, that looks for certain words and phrases to indicate potential problems. Now, what they currently do, is if it's related to terrorism or foreign intelligence, they act upon it. If it's just Mary Sue, afraid for her life from an abusive boyfriend, they ignore that information and file it away. They don't care whether this normal, everyday woman who's just trying to get by lives or dies. I do. I want to make a difference."

"You can't save the entire world, Jones. Trying to is a futile effort. Take it from me. I've been all over it."

"I know that. I'm not trying to save the world. I have no illusions about trying to change the planet or how its people look at each other. I just want to make a difference on my end of it."

"So, what do you need me for?"

"Because I can't do the things you can do. You have a particular set of skills that I can't duplicate. I am good at certain things... computers, finding information, things of that sort. I've always been in the background doing what needs to be done. What I need... is a partner who is good in the field who can do the things you do."

"What makes you think I'm your guy?"

"I've read your file. I know everything about you. You went into the military straight out of high school, became a member of Delta Force, spent eight years in the military, then when your enlistment ended, wound up at the CIA. I know you've been there the last six years, the last four of which you were in a top-secret project called Centurion in which you were a foreign assassin. I also know that Centurion knew you were growing tired of your role in the agency and were seeking to get out, but with all you know about the organization, couldn't just let you leave and sought to terminate you in London six months ago."

"Well then you also know that most of the people that come across my desk have a tendency of ending up dead," Smith said.

Jones shifted his eyes back and forth, "That is something we would have to work on."

"It sounds like you have a noble cause, and I'm all for it, but I'm not sure I'm your guy."

"On the contrary, I believe you're the perfect guy," Jones swallowed more soup.

"I'm a little set in my ways. Violence tends to follow me

around. I'm not a wallflower who believes in turning the other cheek."

"That's where we could benefit each other. I've read your files and reports. You certainly don't run from a fight, and at times seem to embrace it, but it seems like you do it for the right reasons. You don't especially like killing but you will if you have to."

"What are you looking to do? Save people? Send them to the authorities? Jail? What?"

"Whatever the situation calls for, Mr. Smith," Jones replied. "Whatever the situation calls for."

"I have a feeling you're looking for someone who's gonna swoop in and save the day, get the girl, and leave the bad guy tied up and waiting for the police to arrive to take him to the slammer. That ain't me. It's not how I operate."

"I'm fully aware of that. And I'm not naïve enough to think everything we work on will be simple and easy with no grey moral boundaries to cross. I would prefer to do things as quietly and non-violently as possible. In saying that, there will be times when I'll disagree with your methods. And I'm sure there'll be times when I think you're being too violent for the task at hand and I'll be right and you'll be wrong. Just like I'm equally sure they'll be times when I think that... and you'll be right and I'll be wrong and that's exactly what the situation calls for and I just can't see it. But I believe that together we'll complement each other. We won't agree on everything, no. But I think we could be an effective team. If you're of the mind to be one."

Jones stood up, putting on his hat and coat. He

motioned to his two bodyguards that he was done, and they walked over to him.

"Where are you going?" Smith was surprised he was leaving.

"I have other business to attend to."

"I thought we were going over your business."

"It's a lot to take in, I know. I really wasn't expecting to go into so many details with you on our first encounter. I had merely planned to make this an introductory meeting. But things rarely go as planned, don't they?" Jones said.

"How will I contact you if I agree to this venture of yours?"

"Don't worry, Mr. Smith, I'll contact you."

Jones reached into his pocket and took out a piece of paper, putting it down on the table in front of Smith.

"What's this?" Smith smoothed out the slip as he read it.

"I took the liberty of arranging accommodation for you at a nearby hotel. That's your check-in information and room number."

"What makes you think I'll go there?"

"Curiosity. If you're interested in this operation, I assume you'll be there when I check in with you tomorrow. If you're not, then you're not, and I wish you well in your future endeavors."

Smith sat there for a few moments, watching the stranger walk away, followed by his two bodyguards. Once they were out of sight, he glanced down at the piece of paper given to him and thought about the offer. Though he still wasn't sold on the idea, he was intrigued. It would interrupt his plans in Orlando, but Smith knew what he was planning down there wasn't likely to go over well. Jones wanted Smith to help with whatever little crusade he was planning, but if he was as good with computers as he said, and as he appeared, Jones could help Smith as well.

2

S mith was sitting on the bed watching TV when he heard a knock on the door. He went over to the peephole and saw that it was Jones, standing there with a briefcase in his hand. He opened the door and popped his head out, wondering where Jones' guards were.

"Where's the muscle?"

"I didn't feel I had a need for them today,"

"You mean, you no longer feel I might be dangerous to you."

Jones shrugged. "You never know how a first meeting will turn out. If it doesn't go as predicted or planned, precautions must be taken."

"And now you're satisfied that I'm not a sociopathic killer who doesn't care about anything?"

"You're here."

Smith allowed Jones to come in and they sat down at

the small table near the window to continue talking about Jones' business proposition.

"One of the first things we have to do is get you a new identity," Jones stated. "Even if one person inside the CIA knows your Smith alias, it's one too many. Luckily I've brought along several new identities for you to pick from and you can take whichever one you'd like."

"Not necessary. I already have one." Smith smiled in response.

"A new one?"

"One of the things my mentor taught me when I just started out was to create a new identity that nobody else would know, even him, in case things went bad."

"So, nobody else knows it?"

"Only me. And now you."

"What is it?"

Smith went over to his bed and picked up some papers, then placed them in front of Jones for him to look at. "Michael Recker." Jones nodded. "Looks like you have the bases covered. Passport, driver's license, credit cards. Very impressive."

"We're taught to be resourceful."

"So I see."

"I was wondering, how'd you know what plane I was flying in on?" Recker said.

"Flight manifests are rather easy to hack into. The bigger question is why you used one of your known aliases? You must've known the CIA would've been waiting for you down in Florida once your plane arrived."

"I did."

Jones gulped, not knowing how he'd receive his next statement. "The only thing I can deduce is that you were expecting a welcoming committee and weren't actually planning on ever leaving that airport."

Recker smiled. "So how do you plan on financing this operation of yours?"

"I've already taken care of the finances. Money will not be an issue."

"Detective work, security work, vehicles, guns, supplies... all that can add up."

"Believe me, the amount of funds we have at our disposal will not be an issue. I've secured enough money to operate for several years I suspect," Jones said.

"How? Your own money? Or do you have a financial backer in this enterprise of yours?"

"Why does it matter?"

"If you want me to join this operation, I need to know who all the players are. As you can imagine, I don't like surprises."

"There is no one else."

"How much money are we talking? How about my salary?" Recker didn't like to be so mercenary but while the subject was on the table...

"Our starting capital is in excess of five million dollars. Is that enough?"

"To start with. You'll be surprised at how fast that goes. Supplies get expensive. Guns, cars, equipment, payoffs, it adds up quickly."

"I understand your point, Mr. Recker. If the situation

arises that we need more capital, I'm quite confident in my ability to acquire it."

"Are you that wealthy that you have nothing else to do with your money?"

"Why are you so interested in the money?"

"Like I said, I need to know all the players. You want me involved in this operation, then you need to let me know all the details. I'm not just gonna be some hired muscle to do your dirty work and get left out to dry when things go bad," Recker said.

Jones sighed and nodded, realizing he needed to be more forthcoming with the former assassin. "The money has been acquired from some, shall we say, less than reputable citizens."

"You're in bed with criminals?"

"I wouldn't put it quite that way."

"Then how would you put it?"

"The money's stolen," Jones said.

"It's what?"

"I identified some individuals known for criminal activity, mostly drug players, and hacked into their bank accounts. I took around a million from five different people."

"And you think they won't come looking for you?"

"It's not likely." Jones smiled, this was right up his street. "I engineered it to look like the money went into accounts held by their rivals, and sent anonymous messages stating that fact. Meanwhile, the money was siphoned through several other accounts before finding its final resting spot in mine. I used some hacking skills to conceal the final whereabouts of the money. I then went into the rivals' accounts and made it look like they had additional money that they didn't really have."

"So, you're sure they can't trace it back to you?"

"Yes. Each account has a different name on it, in four different countries, so I'm reasonably sure they'd be unable to trace it back to me. As for your salary," Jones reached into his inside pocket which earned a raised eyebrow from Recker. He took a couple of credit cards slowly out of his pocket and put them on the table in front of him. "I've taken the liberty of establishing a bank account for you with an initial amount of one hundred thousand dollars. In addition, on the first of every month, you'll draw a monthly salary of twenty thousand dollars that will automatically go into your account. So, you see Mr. Recker, your salary is also not an issue." He slid the cards across the table with one finger.

"Sounds reasonable enough," Recker said. "How are you going about picking out people that you deem of needing our help? Gonna grab an office building and put up a neon sign?"

Jones grinned. "Not quite what I had in mind. I get the same information the NSA is getting. It's up to me to decipher it. Some people that we'll look into might not actually need the help. But some will."

"I have one condition if I come in on this thing," Recker said.

"OK?"

"I don't help criminals. I won't protect them. I won't save them. If you get something on your computer about one criminal intending to kill another... I won't help them. And I won't get in the way."

"Is that a blanket statement about every person who has a criminal record, Mr. Recker?" Jones raised an eyebrow this time.

"I'm not talking about some twenty-year-old college kid who just got busted for smoking a joint. I'm not talking about someone who got busted for shoplifting once ten years ago. I'm talking seasoned criminals who've got bad rap sheets. Assault, rape, murder. If one gangbanger's trying to kill another one... I'm staying out of it. If you decipher that someone's trying to kill them... let them."

Jones quickly nodded his head, agreeing to Recker's conditions. "Agreed. So, I take it this means you're on board?"

"Let's just say I'm willing to give it a shot and we'll see how it works out."

"Fair enough."

"How many more people do you plan on recruiting on this endeavor?"

"No one. As far as I'm concerned, the less people we have the better. Too many people involved and we risk exposing ourselves. I wish to remain as low key and inconspicuous as possible."

"Probably won't be possible for very long."

"Regardless, let's try to keep it that way."

"When do you anticipate starting this little gig?"

"Oh, we've already started, Mr. Recker," Jones answered, reaching down to the briefcase on the floor and putting it on the table.

Jones unsnapped it and removed a bunch of papers and laid them on the table, looking at them briefly. He then moved the briefcase aside and handed one of the sheets to Recker.

"What's this?" Recker asked, looking the paper over.

"I believe that would be what you call our first...," Jones hesitated, struggling to find the proper wording. "What would you call it exactly? Assignment?"

"Our first person in need?"

Jones smiled, "That'll do for now, I suppose. But yes, that's our first victim or target... neither of those sounds quite right. Anyway, that's who I'd like to help first."

"Why her?"

"Seems like a rather straightforward case. What appears to be a decent woman who's being abused and threatened by an ex-boyfriend. I intercepted several emails, texts, and phone calls indicating he was quite unhappy with the termination of their relationship. Well, as you can see, it's all there for you."

"Why hasn't she just gone to the police?"

"It's a little further down there," Jones said, pointing to it. "But, anyway, she has. She has a protection order out on him."

"They're not worth the paper they're printed on. All it takes is one time for him to violate it and she could be dead by the time the police get there."

"Exactly. She appears to be a good person, no criminal record, works as a nurse at a major hospital, and volunteers for a dog adoption organization. She's in fear for her life from this man and she needs our help."

Recker continued reading the paper on her. On subsequent pages, Jones had included some of the e-mails and texts the boyfriend had sent. Mia Hendricks was twenty-eight years old and worked at St. Mary's Hospital as a pediatric nurse. Three months prior, she'd broken up with her boyfriend of six months over his physical and abusive nature. He had a propensity for drinking too much and caused several bruises on Hendricks' arms, as well as a couple on her face, including a black eye. It was after the black eye that Hendricks' co-workers, fearing for her life, convinced her to get away from him. In the three months they'd been apart, her ex, Stephen Eldridge, hadn't quite gotten the message. He told her that he'd change and not drink anymore, but he was still verbally abusive and threatened to kill her if she didn't get back with him.

"What got her on your radar?" Recker dropped the paper back onto the table and leaned back in his seat.

"Well, anything the software deems a physical threat is noted. Words like kill are an automatic red flag. There are other words and phrases that start sounding alarms, but that's the gist of it. And as you can see, he used that word several times, both in emails and texts."

"Seems like he's not getting the message."

"No, he's not. She keeps rebuffing him, but with each subsequent contact, Eldridge's replies are getting more dangerous and indicating he won't stop no matter what."

"So, what do you want me to do? Throw him off a rooftop?"

"Uh... while I have no doubt in the effectiveness of

such a strategy, I was hoping for something a little less... noticeable," Jones said.

"Would you rather me whisper sweet little nothings in his ear?"

Jones opened his mouth to speak, then closed it again as his eyes danced around, thinking of a proper reply. "I was hoping you could get him to realize the error of his ways and divert his attention to a different path."

"I thought you'd let me work things through my way?"

"Merely a suggestion, Mr. Recker. Maybe try my way first..."

"And then throw him off the rooftop?"

"I'd prefer our first case to not wind up with a dead body."

"Well aren't we picky?" Recker smiled at his own joke.

They discussed Hendricks and her situation for a few more minutes before Recker stood up, ready to start moving. He put on his long, grey trench coat.

"Where are you going?" Jones said.

"Need guns and ammunition. Have to be properly equipped in case something happens." Recker shrugged the coat onto his shoulders and patted his pockets.

"How much money do you think you'll need?"

"Not sure. Have to find someone first."

"Can't you just get them from a dealer?"

"Not the kind of dealer I'm looking for."

"You mean criminals? The very same people we're trying to put away?"

"Well, buying the stuff we'll need, you can't just walk into a store and ask for a bunch of guns and put it on the credit card," Recker said. "Those stores have cameras. I think it's a good idea if we try to avoid video surveillance. Plus, you need to fill out forms, and the guns are registered. If you want to stay under the radar, you need guns that are untraceable and avoid putting your name to anything."

"Sounds logical."

"Plus there's only so much you can learn from computers and emails and such. Sometimes you need good old-fashioned intelligence. Eyes and ears on the street. Connections. Most decent people won't have the kind of information we'll need sometimes."

"Well, I'll take your word for it I suppose. Although I do appreciate your thoroughness, I did establish new identities for us to use so that wouldn't be a problem."

"Trust me. I've tracked people down for a living for the past eight years. If you leave a paper trail, eventually someone will find you. No matter how careful and deceptive you think you are. If you leave a crumb, someone will eventually find it. It's best to stick to using cash, staying out of cameras, and not filling out forms that can leave a trace."

"I will agree with your judgment on the matter."

"How will I contact you?"

"I took the liberty of acquiring phones. They're prepaid to avoid detection," Jones said. "I already programmed my number in yours."

"Good. One other thing... we're gonna need a base of operations to work in. Don't tell me you're planning on doing this out of a hotel room or a bedroom or something."

"On the contrary, Mr. Recker. I've acquired a little business just outside the city where we can set up."

"A business?"

"A legitimate business on the first floor and office space on the second."

"Are you sure that's wise?" Recker didn't want this thing to fall at the first hurdle.

"Of course. It wouldn't look good if two men were seen going into a vacant warehouse or building all the time, would it?"

"I suppose not."

"I'm the legitimate owner of a business and I have every right to use that office for whatever purpose I see fit. Who'd think twice?" Jones said.

"You're probably right. What kind of business is it, anyway?"

Jones wrote down the address on a piece of paper and handed it to Recker. "Here's the address. You'll see when you get there. There's a private entrance in the back with steps leading up to it."

"OK."

"Oh, Mr. Recker?" Jones said, remembering something.

Recker had just gotten out the door when he heard Jones call for him. He came back into the room and saw Jones taking keys out of his pocket and holding them in front of him.

"I almost forgot," Jones said, handing the keys over.

"What's this for?"

"Well it's tough to get around the city on foot or by public transportation. So, I took the liberty of acquiring a car. An SUV to be exact. A brand new black Ford Explorer with tinted windows is in the parking lot."

"Company car?" Recker said with a smile.

"On the contrary, it's yours."

"Mine? Gonna take it out of my salary?"

"No. Consider it a signing bonus."

Recker nodded. "Thanks, Jones."

"I'm gonna stay here for a few more minutes and check a few things on Ms. Hendricks. After that I'll head back to the office. There's still a few more things that need to be settled there."

"All right. After I've... done what I need to do, I'll meet you over there."

"Sounds like a plan."

"By the way, you can save me a little time. Where would you suggest I go to meet some rough-looking characters who might, by chance, have some guns?"

"There are several areas. You could try Hunting Park, that's North Philly between second and ninth I believe. Or you could go a little farther until you hit Germantown. Or there's Kensington. Or..."

"Basically, what you're telling me is just drive into the city and park anywhere."

"There are a lot of good parts to this city, Mr. Recker. Most areas are good. But there's a few that's not. You asked for the not so nice ones."

"Do me a favor and lock up when you're done?" Recker

said. "Unless you, by chance, took the liberty of acquiring a house or an apartment for me as well?"

"Oh, thank you for reminding me," Jones said, grinning. He tossed another set of keys toward Recker that he snagged out of the air. "It's a nice little apartment, quiet community, you should like it."

Recker returned the smile and continued out the door. He went to the parking lot to find the new truck that he'd just received. He hit the alarm button on his keypad, saw the lights blinking on a truck parked on the far right of the lot and heard the horn sound. He walked over to it, got in, checked out the interior and fiddled around with some of the controls.

"This gig might not be so bad after all."

3

Recker drove through the city for a couple of hours, just trying to familiarize himself with his surroundings. He'd been in Philadelphia before about five years prior to this, but only for a few days, and he really didn't get to see much of the city. He'd have to rely on Jones, at least for a little while, to get him familiar with the place.

He did take Jones' advice and drove around through Hunting Park. It was a rough-looking area. He turned onto sixth street near an elementary school, a three-story brick building with a raised basement. He parked near the curb as he saw several youthful looking guys in the school playground area.

Recker watched them for a few minutes, looking like they were buying and selling drugs, as money and small bags passed between the parties. He waited until they finished their business until he made his move.

Recker fixated on one guy and as the group broke up,

he got out of his car and started walking towards him. The other four guys went separate ways. Recker looked back to make sure they were still going in the opposite direction. He started closing in on his target and picked up his pace. The guy he was following had a suspicion he was being tailed and turned his head back, seeing Recker coming towards him. He darted across the street towards a mini-mart, Recker running after him. Recker anticipated he'd run and had already begun in that direction before the guy even took off. Recker grabbed the collar of the man's jacket and pushed him into the wall of the building.

"Yo, man, what'd you do that for?" the man asked, turning around to face his attacker.

"Just want some information, sonny."

"What're you, a cop?"

"Nope."

"You look like a cop," the man said, noting Recker's hairstyle and the way he dressed. "You in narcotics or somethin'?"

"I'm not a cop." Recker tightened his grip.

"Well if you're not a cop then what you want with me? You're in the wrong neighborhood, pal."

"Looking for some information. I figured you were the guy that could give it to me," Recker said, taking his hands off the guy.

"Got the wrong guy, dude. I don't know nothin'."

Recker smiled. "Oh, I think you do."

"If you ain't a cop then what you want information for?"

"What's your name?"

"Why should I tell you?"

"Because I'm asking."

The man looked at Recker, wondering what he was up to. He didn't look like the usual kind of guy that was in that neighborhood.

"I need to do some business," Recker said when the name wasn't forthcoming. "You look like the kind of guy that can help me do that."

"That all depends. What kind of business you talking about?"

"I need weapons. Unregistered and untraceable," Recker said, looking around to make sure nobody else was nearby.

"What you need weapons for?"

"That's my business."

"How do I know you're not a cop just looking to set me up or something?"

"If I was a cop, I'd have busted you and your friends back there for dealing. I'm not a cop. Now can you help me or not?"

"Maybe. Whatcha need?"

"A few handguns, assault rifles, maybe a few grenades, a missile launcher'd be nice," Recker told him.

The man's eyes widened, surprised at the request. "What're you, trying to start a war?"

"Nope. Just like to be prepared."

"Prepared for what?"

"Like I said, that's my business. Can you help me or not?"

"Uh... yeah, I might know some people."

"I would like to have it within the next few days if you can arrange it."

"You got the money ready if I can?"

"Money's not an object. If you can get something set up for tomorrow, I'll give you a little something extra for your troubles," Recker said. "I also prefer Glocks and Sig Sauers if you can get them."

The man moved his head around like he was thinking. "Aight. I'll let you know."

"Give me a call on this number when you're ready," Recker said, handing him a paper with his number on it.

The man nodded, "A'ight."

"One more thing... I don't do business with people I don't know. So, what's your name?"

"Tyrell."

"Tyrell what?"

"Gibson. You didn't tell me your name yet."

"You can call me Recker."

"Recker? That a nickname or something?"

Recker shook his head, "No."

"That's a fitting name then, 'cause it seems like you're the kind of guy who likes to wreck things."

"Yeah. Almost like I picked the name myself or something."

"You like a mobster or somethin'?"

"If I was a mobster, do you think I'd be here asking you about guns?"

"No. I guess not."

"I'll be waiting for your call."

"Just to warn you, these guys I'll talk to about the guns,

they're not the kind of people you mess with. You better not be yanking their chain or try to cheat them with money or anything. You better have it. Or else. You don't wanna mess with them."

"Same could be said for me." Recker smiled.

"I dunno man, you're like all calm and shit, but there's something crazy about you."

"Glad you noticed."

Recker ended the conversation and went back to his truck. He looked at the address that Jones gave to him and plugged it into the GPS in the truck. It was in Bensalem, a large suburb located just outside of the city. He took the I-95 highway to get there, arriving at the strip center business in about half an hour. There were five businesses located in the shopping center, a pharmacy, a pizza place, a self-serve laundromat, a real estate office, and an insurance office. Recker stood there by his truck, looking over the small complex. He looked at the address on the signs of the businesses until he saw the one he was looking for. He wasn't sure what to make of it. The type of business they were running was sitting overtop of a laundromat?

"This is a new one," he said to himself.

He made his way around to the back of the building and walked up the wooden steps to the second floor. Recker turned the knob, but it was locked. He knocked on the door and heard movement inside. The door opened just a sliver, with only one of Jones' eyes visible. As soon as he saw it was Recker, he opened it further and let him in.

"Glad to see you made it," Jones said. "Find the place alright?"

"Yeah, no problems. You really think having this place over a laundromat is appropriate?"

"Why not? It's a perfect cover. A legitimate business. People coming and going all the time. But it's not something that needs hands on management to run, letting us focus our attention on the more important matters that we have to attend to."

"What if a machine breaks down? You doing the repairs?" Recker said, his question dripping with sarcasm. He didn't think Jones liked to get his hands dirty... in any sense.

"Don't be silly, Mr. Recker. I've hired someone to look after the place every couple of days, clean, make repairs and such."

Recker was walking around the room, sizing up the office. He was a little surprised at how it looked. He anticipated some dingy lit room with an antique desk, maybe a lamp, and one or two computers. What he found was what seemed like a very high-tech establishment. Brightly lit, a huge L-shaped desk that had six computers on it, three of which were laptops. There were maps of the area on a wall, a big whiteboard on another one, as well as two microfiber couches.

"How do you like it?" Jones wondered.

"I'm impressed. I wasn't picturing something so involved. When you first told me about all this, I thought it might be some rinky-dink operation out of your mom's basement or something."

"Hardly."

"I'm gonna need something to house the guns and weapons we'll need."

"About that... do you really think it's going to be necessary to have all these weapons you're talking about?"

"If you wanna help people, then you're gonna have to be prepared for whatever we might come across. What if I'm protecting someone? Bullet-proof vest would be nice. Night stake out? Night vision goggles would sure do the trick. It'd be easy to come back here and grab what's needed for the assignment. If not, you might not always get the chance to go out and acquire those types of things," Recker said. "They don't just sell that stuff at the local supermarket you know."

Jones nodded. "Your point's been made. What size will you need?"

Recker walked over to the desk and found a pen and some paper. He jotted down a few ideas and drawings and handed it to his new partner. Jones looked at it for a few minutes.

"I'll see what I can do," Jones said.

"The sooner the better. I'll probably be able to start stocking it tomorrow."

"Have something lined up with whoever you were seeking earlier?"

"We'll see. Looks promising though," Recker said. "Can you run a check on a Tyrell Gibson?"

"Should be able to. Might take a few minutes," Jones said, sitting down at one of the laptops. "I'll run the name through the DMV so we can get a photo so you can verify."

"You can hack the DMV?"

"I can get into just about anything. Some things are easier than others, of course. Is this the guy you're getting your equipment from?"

"More like the third party connecting two interested people together."

They waited a few minutes before a match popped up, showing Gibson's driver license photo and information.

"That's him," Recker stated. "Let's get whatever else we can on him."

"Why? For what purpose?"

"He might be of some use to us. If he's got eyes and ears on everything happening on the street, he might be someone I can pump for information if the need arises."

"I'll tap into police records."

"Seems a little sketchy, Jones. Hacking into all these databases. Some might say you're no better than the people you're trying to put away."

"Hardly, Mr. Recker. You could scarcely compare a rapist, a child abuser, a murderer, an assault perpetrator, or someone of that ilk, to me, who's simply acquiring information."

"Sounds like the rationale of a criminal, spinning whatever lawbreaking thing you're doing to suit your own tastes and needs." Recker was taking his chance to shake Jones' chains.

Jones sat back and spun his chair around, a little perturbed at what he deemed to be ridiculous accusations. While he knew he was breaking multiple laws by hacking into private government databases, he felt since he was doing so with good intentions; it wasn't as egregious an offense as it looked, though he knew others would not have the same outlook as he did. He said as much to Recker.

"I am not doing anything that the NSA hasn't done, or won't do. They've done the same things that I'm doing, only on a much larger scale," Jones said.

"I'm just messing with you. With the things I've done, I'm hardly in a position to be critiquing other people's judgments," Recker said holding up both hands in submission.

Jones spun his chair back around and focused on his work again, pulling up what he could find on Gibson. He appeared to be a small-time criminal, no major offenses to his name. From what Jones could gather, Gibson didn't appear to be a part of any gang that he could trace. He seemed to operate on his own.

"Here's what you're looking for," Jones said.

Recker pulled his chair alongside the computer genius. "How's he looking?"

"He appears to have a modest record. Nothing major though. Mostly petty crimes. Shoplifting, robbery, theft, receiving stolen property, pick pocketing, fraud, and smuggling. Longest he spent in jail was twelve months. No hard time, just local facilities. No known gang affiliations."

"That's good."

"Why?"

"If he's affiliated with a gang, it's unlikely he'd be any help to us at all. If he's a loner, or just small time, it's more likely he'd be willing to talk," Recker concentrated on the details on screen.

"When do you expect to deal with him?"

"He's gonna call me later if he has a deal set up. Hopefully for tomorrow."

While Jones continued pouring over the information that was on the laptop, Recker looked over at one of the other computers, which had a picture of Ms. Hendricks on it. He reread some of her information, before going back to her picture. He stared at it for a few minutes; her face reminding him of someone he once knew. As he looked at it, his memory went back to London, six months ago, replaying the events in his mind.

"Centurion Six, are you in position?" The voice crackled in his ear.

"I'm just outside the office building now. Going in," Smith said into his sleeve.

"We got word his assistants left an hour ago so he should be alone."

"Roger that."

"Check back in when the job's finished."

Smith entered the building through a side entrance, which was left unlocked by a security guard, just as was planned. The guard unlocked it just five minutes prior to that, right before he took a coffee break. Smith glided through the hallway until he reached the stairs in the middle of the building. Roger Coleman was supposed to be the intended target, one of the more influential members of the London Assembly.

Just like every other mission, Smith had no clue why his victim's number was up. Didn't know what Coleman did, or why he was chosen to be eliminated. All Smith knew was the job at hand. He went up to the fifth floor where Coleman's office was located and went down the hall to the fourth door on the left. Smith couldn't see through the frosted glass door but did notice that a small light was on in the office. He took a quick look around, double checked his gun, a Sig Sauer 1911-.22 caliber pistol, took a deep breath, turned the handle, opened the door, then burst through the entrance. He quickly found the desk and was ready to fire, but found no one sitting there. Smith looked around the room, not seeing a sign of life anywhere. He walked around the other side of the desk and looked underneath. It wouldn't have been the first time he found his victim hiding under one. He didn't hear a single sound, unusual from someone who was either hiding, or trying to get away. Usually he'd hear heavy breathing, footsteps, or something breaking accidentally from trying to run. It was eerily quiet. The lamp on the desk was on but Smith took a closer look at the desk. It struck him as odd. It was very neat. Too neat for someone who was working late. There was a file folder on the top left corner of the desk but that was it. No disheveled papers all thrown about, no scattered pens or pencils, nothing that'd indicate someone was there.

"Alpha One, we have a negative on our target," Smith said. "He's not here."

Smith waited about thirty seconds before trying to repeat the message. Once again, it went without a reply.

He looked around the room again, alarm bells going off in his head. He quietly walked over to the door, listening for any sounds in the hallway. Thinking he may have been set up, he had a feeling someone was out there waiting for him. But he had no other options, he had to take the chance and leave sometime. Smith slipped out the door and started walking down the hallway, paying careful attention to his surroundings. He believed a person could just as easily run into trouble by going too fast and not paying attention, as you could by maintaining a steady pace. He thought it was more beneficial to know what was around you as it was to go quickly.

Just as he passed one of the other offices, he heard the elevator chiming. He snapped his body around as the elevator doors opened, ready for someone to step off. Nobody did. He took a few more steps toward it when the door by the stairs swung open, a man immediately opening up and firing. Smith instantly went down from the blow of the first bullet, lodging into his stomach. He rolled on the floor and returned fire, hitting his attacker several times as they each emptied their pistols. Holding his stomach, blood soaking his hand, he reached around and grabbed another magazine to reload his pistol.

Smith got to his feet, grimacing in pain as he slowly walked over to the other man lying on the ground. With the gun laying close to the man's hand, Smith kicked the gun down the hall. Smith nudged him with his foot a couple of times, and after satisfying himself he was dead, checked his pockets for some ID. He had none on him. He saw he had an earpiece, the wire going into the back of the shirt down to back of his pants. Smith turned him over and took the earpiece out and listened to see if he could pick up anything. After a minute, a voice spoke out.

"Centurion Twenty-One, have you finished your assignment?"

It was the same voice that gave him his own orders. Smith thought about whether he should answer, and all the different things he could answer with, or just ignore it. If he didn't reply, they'd know the agent failed. If Smith replied in the wrong manner, they'd also know they failed to eliminate him. He picked up the earpiece and waited for them to ask again.

"Centurion Twenty-One, is your assignment complete?"

"This is Twenty-One, mission successful. Target's been eliminated."

"Good job. Go back to your hotel and wait for instructions."

"Roger that."

Smith went down the stairs quickly, knowing he didn't have a lot of time, but also knowing that there may have been more than one agent sent there for him. Once he reached the bottom of the stairs he slowed down, hearing what sounded like someone pacing just outside the door. He knew it wasn't the guard since he shouldn't return for another hour. Holding the side of his stomach, still bleeding profusely, he closed his eyes and took a deep breath. Smith pushed the door open, his gun already raised and in firing position. He immediately saw another agent standing there and began firing, three shots landing in the agent's chest before he could get a shot away. Smith did a three sixty in the lobby just in case anyone else was there waiting, but without having to duck any other bullets, assumed it was just the two of them. He ducked back out the side entrance and made his getaway through some bushes and trees, not knowing what was on the other side of them.

Knowing he couldn't go back to his hotel room in fear that the agency had someone watching it just in case, Smith wasn't sure where else he could go. The agency had contacts everywhere, and anyone that he knew of, could burn him. He didn't know who he could trust, if anybody. After about ten minutes, he walked out of the clump of trees. Suddenly, his thoughts turned to his girlfriend, Carrie.

Worried that they might not have been satisfied with just taking him out and might try to eliminate anyone close to him, he got out his cell phone and tried calling her. She was the only person who really mattered to him, who he thought they might try to take out. He had no other close friends. His parents had both passed away several years ago, and being an only child, was never close with any other relatives.

Smith dialed Carrie's number, desperate to reach her and hear her voice, letting him know she was OK. With the time difference, Smith figured she should've gotten home from work about a half hour ago. Her phone kept ringing, eventually going to voicemail. Smith kept walking, trying the number again. This time, after four rings, the phone was answered. She didn't talk though or greet him with the usual warm hello that she usually did, heightening Smith's fears.

"Carrie?"

A man's voice answered back. "I'm afraid Carrie will not be able to come to the phone right now."

"What have you done to her?"

"I wouldn't worry about her so much as I would about yourself."

"I swear if you hurt her, I will hunt you down and kill you," Smith said, his heart racing.

"Big threat from a man who won't make it through the night."

"Let Carrie go. You have no beef with her. If it's me you want, come and get me."

"It's not really necessary at this point. I'm afraid you'll never see her again."

"Don't do this to her. She's a good person."

"She seems that way. Too bad she fell for a man like you. That was her undoing."

Fearing for her life, Smith was ready to bargain. "I'll give myself up for her."

"How chivalrous of you."

"I mean it. My life for hers. Let her go and I'll turn myself in to whoever and wherever you want. Just tell me where."

"If only you had called ten minutes ago. I would've made the exchange in a heartbeat. I'm afraid now... it's not possible," the man said cryptically.

"Why not?" Smith asked, stopping in his tracks, afraid of what he was about to hear.

"Because five minutes ago... I killed poor, sweet Carrie. Don't worry though. I gave her the professional courtesy of making it quick and painless. She never saw it coming."

Smith hunched over like he was about to throw up, though he didn't. He straightened up again, though still wincing from the pain of the gunshot wound.

"You didn't have to do that! She was innocent!" Smith yelled.

"Nobody's innocent."

"She didn't have to die! If you wanted me, come get me!"

"Oh, we will. We will."

"Who are you? I'd like to know so I can make your death extra special when I look into your eyes."

The man laughed, amused by the threats of a man he assumed would soon be dead. "Seventeen," he said then the line went dead.

A whirlwind of thoughts swirled around in Smith's head. Carrie was dead. Because of him. If she'd never have met him, she'd still be alive. Smith eventually got to a sidewalk and continued walking along the street, not really having a destination in mind. He closed his coat tightly to prevent his wound from showing to passers-by. For more than two hours he wandered around the streets of London, putting his head down, and not going anywhere in particular. He knew Centurion had people on the ground looking for him by now so he couldn't go to anyone he already knew. Even if there were people he could trust, which there wasn't, he wouldn't put anyone else's lives at risk. Not for him.

He knew he left a fair amount of blood at the shootout at the office so he figured they'd check hospitals and any underground doctors in the area first. When the third hour after the shootout had passed, Smith finally picked his head up and looked around, amazingly finding himself standing in front of a hospital. He debated whether he wanted to go in. He wasn't sure if he should go in. He wasn't sure if he even wanted to go in. With Carrie gone, he thought maybe he'd just give up and join her wherever she now was. He thought maybe it was better if he just kept moving, or creeped off down some dark alley, knowing eventually he'd collapse.

Then he thought about Carrie and knew she'd want him to carry on. His legs began moving, and he walked through the hospital doors, taking a seat. He wasn't sure if he was doing it for Carrie, or for himself. Thoughts of rage and revenge flowed through him. If he gave up, he wouldn't be able to extract the punishment that Centurion and especially seventeen had coming to them. He found the waiting area for the emergency room and saw an empty chair towards the back and sat down.

"Mr. Recker? Mr. Recker?" Jones said, touching his shoulder.

Recker broke free of his stare, the combination of hearing his name and feeling Jones' hand, woke him from his trance. He snapped his head towards Jones, still in a little bit of a haze.

"Are you OK?" Jones' face showed his concern.

"Yeah. Yeah. I'm fine," Recker replied, getting the images out of his head.

"I'm sorry. I hope I didn't interrupt anything important for you. You seemed to be in some sort of trance."

Recker shook his head, "No, it's fine. Just thinking about something."

"Anything you'd like to talk about?"

"Uh... no. No, I'm good."

Jones had a feeling he was replaying the events of something terrible in his mind. London, or one of the other couple of dozen assassinations he'd been involved with. Or something unrelated to any of them. Jones couldn't be sure what it was, but whatever it was, it had to be something traumatic for him as he seemed troubled by whatever he was thinking about.

Recker and Carrie had been dating for a little under two years. They met in Orlando, where Carrie lived, running into each other in a hotel lobby where Recker was staying. It was just a layover for him, in between jobs, whereas she was there for a conference for her job. While she was on a break between sessions, they sat next to each other on a bench and began talking. Well, she did most of the talking. He was hesitant to talk and get to know anybody, knowing he wasn't likely to see them again. Eventually, with her pleasant personality, she got him to open up a little. He told her he worked for the government and went overseas often. After that conference, they exchanged phone numbers and agreed to see each other again.

Every chance Recker got from that day forward, he

traveled down to Orlando to be with her, usually for one or two weeks a month, though a couple of times he had as much as four weeks to spend with her while he waited for an assignment. He tried to shield her from what he did as much as he could. It wasn't until three months before London happened that he sat down with her and explained exactly what he did and who he was. Up until then, he felt like he was leading her on and thought she was going down a path with someone that wasn't real. He fully expected her to be done with him after he told her the truth about him and was hoping she would be, wanting Carrie to find a nicer and more stable guy than he was that could really make her happy. She deserved at least that much. Her response wasn't what he envisioned.

She'd always known he was hiding something about his work but she never wanted to pry. From her vantage point, he was a handsome, kind, considerate, caring guy who she wanted to spend the rest of her life with. Whatever he did for a living, it wasn't the person that she knew. It wasn't the person that he was when they were together. She understood that he did things for the government that weren't pretty, that most people wouldn't understand, or couldn't stomach.

From that moment on, Recker questioned his role in the agency. He expected, and had fully accepted, the fact that he was likely to spend the rest of his life alone and would die in a hail of gunfire. But her love changed his perspective. He now had something, and someone, to live for.

Recker and Carrie had discussed him leaving the

agency, and though she never forced him to do so, he wanted to quit. Though Carrie was happy that he was making that decision, she didn't want him to do it on her account. She wanted him to do it because he was ready to, and not because he felt like she was forcing him to. But now that he had her, Recker wanted to give it all up and just settle down to spend all his time with her.

He'd approached a couple of his superiors a month before the London assignment and expressed his feelings to them, telling them that he wanted out. Though Recker expected to hear some objections to his leaving, and wondered about how they would take it, they never expressed any negativity to him. Not one bad word, leaving him to think they were OK with it. They led him to believe that he would be able to leave the agency behind and have a normal life.

Obviously, he was wrong, and as far as he was concerned, was likely never to forgive himself for leading Carrie down the path that eventually got her killed.

4

R ecker had just walked into the office, two empty duffel bags draped over his shoulders crisscrossed. Jones was sitting at the desk working and turned around. His eyes widened, wondering how much equipment Recker was bringing back.

"Just how many guns are you planning on purchasing, Mr. Recker?"

"Huh? Oh. These aren't both for the guns. One's to put the money in. You have it ready?"

"Twenty thousand dollars. Just as you requested. It's over there in the corner in the briefcase."

Recker walked over to it, shuffling the money from the briefcase into one of the duffel bags. Gibson called Recker first thing in the morning to let him know he had a dealer ready to deliver if he was still interested in purchasing the weapons. Jones had a medium size safe in the office, holding about fifty thousand dollars. His goal was to have a large amount of cash on hand to avoid frequent trips to the bank. Since banks had cameras, they thought it was best not to be seen there much, if at all.

Gibson said the deal would happen along sixty ninth street. There were some vacant stores in a strip center where a McDonald's was located. The deal would happen on Barrington, the street behind the center, inside a vacant, boarded up row home. They'd have a red flag or bandana on one of the boarded-up windows to let Recker know which house it was.

"Do you need me to accompany you or help you in any way?" Jones offered but hoped the answer was no.

"Thanks. But I don't think you'll be much help in this instance."

Jones breathed a quiet sigh of relief. "You don't think it's a trap do you? Nothing could go wrong, right?"

"Something could always go wrong. Could be they just decide to try and kill me and take the cash and forget about the deal." Recker shrugged. "Wouldn't be the first time that happened."

"Maybe it's best if you try to acquire the weapons in some other manner then?"

"No, I don't think that'll be necessary."

"Why not?"

"Because once they see that I could become a long-term customer, the possibility of future, larger payments should outweigh this one smaller transaction," Recker said with a grin.

"You call twenty thousand dollars a small transaction?"

"It is in this instance."

Recker stewed around the office for another hour, just

passing the time until he had to leave. Once the meeting time started creeping up, he grabbed his gun, tucked it inside his pants and put his coat on. He put his earpiece in so he could communicate with Jones if he should have to.

"Please be careful," Jones said.

Recker stopped as he reached the door and turned around. "You almost sound concerned." He smiled.

"I am. I'd hate to have to go through this process all over again if something happened to you."

Recker smiled at his sense of humor, dry as it was. Like his own. It took him about forty-five minutes to get to sixty ninth street. This area was technically in Upper Darby but it was only a few minutes outside Philadelphia. He found the McDonald's and turned onto Barrington. It wasn't a large street and only had a dozen or so houses on it. It only took him a minute to find the one with the red bandana pinned to a boarded-up window, even though it wasn't necessary, as there was only one house on the street with any boarded windows at all. The other houses appeared to be well maintained. Recker parked on the street along the curb, seeing several other cars in the driveway. He grabbed the empty duffel bag, as well as the one with the money, and slung them over his shoulder as he got out of his truck.

As Recker approached the house, the front door swung open, with a young, rugged looking man appearing in the frame of the door. Recker stopped for a second then continued toward the door, walking past the unfriendly looking man. Recker immediately saw a large table in the middle of the room with a few folding chairs surrounding it. There were six other men around the edges of the table on the far side, a few of them Recker could see with guns tucked in the front of their pants. One of those men was Gibson. Recker couldn't see if he was armed. Gibson walked around the table and stopped halfway between Recker and the man who'd be selling him the guns.

"This is Recker, the man I was telling you about," Gibson said.

"Before we get started, if I hear a siren outside or anything, I'll be gone long before they get inside. I got men upstairs lookin' out," the leader said.

"I don't want the police here anymore than you do," Recker said.

"Whatcha want the guns for?"

"That's my business," Recker stood his ground, alert to what was happening around him.

"If you intend to use them in my city, then it's my business too."

"Oh? Did you get elected mayor recently?" Recker just couldn't help himself sometimes.

"Don't be cute. You know who I am?"

Recker shrugged. "Haven't a clue. Does it matter?"

The leader looked at Gibson, not sure he believed him. The man at the door came into the room, standing a few feet behind Recker, just in case anything went down.

"Vincent send you here?" the leader said.

"No idea who that is."

"The Italians?"

Recker shrugged again. "Still no clue. Look, if you don't wanna sell me the guns, that's fine. I'll just be on my way, and I'll do my business elsewhere. Maybe I'll look up this Vincent you're talking about."

Recker turned as if he was about to walk away when the leader stopped him. "Alright man, just calm down. I gotta take precautions as to who I do business with. If you don't know who those other chumps are, then you must not be from around here."

"I'm not."

"Where you from?"

"Around."

"What are you planning on doing with the guns?"

"My business," Recker said, repeating his answer with a shake of his head.

The leader pulled one of the metal folding chairs out and sat down, sizing up the stranger in front of him. "You're not like the usual people who come in here."

"Is that a compliment?"

The man shrugged. "Somethin' different about you. Somethin' dangerous. How do I know if I sell you these guns you ain't gonna use them to come after me or take out my crew?"

"Well... stay out of my way and you got nothing to worry about."

"You got the cash on you?"

Recker opened up the duffel bag and lowered it so he could see it was in there.

"I could just kill you and take the money and keep the guns for myself," the leader said, the threat clear.

"Maybe. Big gamble for you though."

"How's that?"

"Well, if I hear so much as a twitch from that guy behind me, or anything that sounds like he's pulling that gun out of his pants, the first thing I'm gonna do is blow a hole through your head. Then I'll turn around for him. I should be able to take out one or two more of you before you get your wish though." Recker smiled at the man opposite him.

The man smiled back, impressed with Recker's confidence. "You're very sure of yourself. I like that. You come in here, someone who's not from around here, and you have the balls to make threats about killing me and my men."

"I don't make idle threats. I back them up," Recker said, beginning to get aggravated.

"I believe you. You're very calm for someone in a difficult situation. Lot of money, guns, outnumbered, but you don't seem worried at all. Your life could be in danger and you don't even look like you're breaking a sweat."

"The only people who fear for their life when it's in danger... are the people who have something to lose."

The man nodded, understanding what he was saying. "You a cop?"

"Nope."

"Ex-cop?"

"No."

"Well you somethin'. Military?"

Recker sighed, still weary of the questions. "Used to be."

"So, what are you now?"

"Nothing. Look, we doing this deal or not? Because if

you ask me one more question I'm gonna walk out that door."

The man nodded to one of his men, who left the room with another member of the gang. They returned a couple of minutes later, bringing with them several large bags containing weapons, dumping them on the table for Recker to see. There must have been close to a hundred guns laying on the table, pistols, revolvers, rifles, of all different makes and models.

"I charge a little less than double retail on most. The Glocks are a thousand each. Sig rifles two thousand each. Sig pistols fifteen hundred, except the 250's which are a thousand," the leader informed. "Even got an AK-47 at the end there, that's fifteen hundred."

"Sounds fair," Recker said, throwing him the bag of money.

"Just take whichever ones you want. Gibs'll count the cost. I won't get picky if you're a little over."

Recker looked the pile over, picking a few up to get a feel for each weapon as well as test the sights out on them. After a few minutes of deliberating on which ones he wanted, he finally decided.

"I'll take the full and subcompact 250's. Three Glocks," Recker said, putting them in the empty duffel bag. "The AK-47..." he looked over the rest of the guns laid out before him. "Three of the Sig pistols. And four of the rifles. What's that come to, Tyrell?"

"Uh... nineteen thou," Gibson answered.

"Got a thousand left to play with," the leader said as he rocked back in the chair.

Recker looked up and down the table before noticing a couple of silencers toward the end, nestled in between a pair of guns. "How much are the silencers?"

"Normally a thousand each. Because we're getting off on a good foot here, I'll let you take two if you want, one for the rifle and one for the pistol, and we'll call it even."

"Generous of you," Recker said, grabbing the two silencers and shoving them in the bag.

"With a haul like that, I'm assuming I'll be hearing about you in the coming weeks."

"Maybe," Recker said. He turned to leave then did an about face. "Oh, uh, one more thing... I like to know the names of who I'm doing business with. I never did get yours."

The leader hesitated, unsure if he should give it, though he finally relented. "Jeremiah."

"Good," Recker said, turning to leave again, and again turning back. "I guess it's two more things. I have a few other articles for my wish list. Can you get some grenades, maybe an RPG, night vision, tear gas, tasers... oh..." Recker laughed. "And a bullet-proof vest."

Jeremiah looked at him like he was a little crazy asking for all those items. "What're you, trying to start a war or something?"

Recker smiled. "One might think so."

"I'll look into it."

"Good. If you get something, let me know. Gibbs has my number," Recker said, walking out the door.

"I told you, Jeremiah, somethin' ain't right about him," Gibson said.

Jeremiah went over to the door and watched Recker get into his truck and drive away.

"We'll try to keep tabs on him if we can," Jeremiah told his crew. "If anything happens to any of our boys over the next few weeks, and it's done by someone matching his description, we'll know what's what."

Once Recker got back to the office, he put the duffel bag of guns down in the corner of the room. Jones broke free of his computer work and was a bit concerned about the bag full of weapons.

"I do hope you plan on putting them in a more secure location," Jones said.

"Yep. Soon as I get some type of safe or cabinet constructed."

"I assume all went as expected?"

"Yep."

"Get all you need?"

"Not quite. Still a few more items I'd like to have around," Recker said.

"How much did you get?"

"Let's see... there was eight pistols, four rifles... and an AK-47."

"Oh, dear."

"And a couple of silencers."

"And you still need more?"

"You wanna do this right, you need to be prepared. We're good with guns for the moment. Just accessories that we need."

"Oh."

Recker sat down at one of the desktops and started

looking at gun cabinets. After a few minutes, he decided on which one he wanted. It was a large steel one that could hold up to fifty guns, plus shelving for some of the accessories, such as ammo, cameras, tasers, and such. Plus, there were pouches on the inside of the door that could hold the pistols, as well as the silencers, scopes, and other small items.

"Find one to your liking?" Jones' eyes never left his screen.

"This one should do."

"When do you plan on acquiring it?"

"No time like the present," Recker said.

"At the risk of seeming to be impatient, when were you planning on working on Ms. Hendrick's case?"

"Oh. That. Yeah, I guess I should get started on that."

"It might be helpful. Especially considering I intercepted his latest text message about two hours ago, telling her that if he couldn't have her, then nobody else would either," Jones said.

"Have you any idea where Eldridge is at right now?"

"Should be at work. He's done in about an hour."

"I'll let you know how it goes. Get me that safe."

Recker immediately left to meet Eldridge before he left work. He worked in construction, for a large company, and was on a job in the northeast part of the city in Mayfair. As Recker was driving, Jones texted him Eldridge's exact location. It only took Recker about half an hour to get to the construction site. He parked on the street and stared at the site, watching different workers come and go. Jones sent him a picture of Eldridge to make sure he recognized him.

He patiently waited for an hour and a half for the crew to finish work. They worked a little later than usual since they were behind schedule on the building. Though there were still some guys working, it looked like Eldridge had finished for the day since he had his coat on and keys in hand. As he walked toward his pickup, he hit the button to unlock it, flicking the lights on and off. Recker looked at the picture on his phone to confirm it was him. He quickly exited his car and walked in his target's direction, making sure he didn't get away from him. Recker timed it just right. As soon as Eldridge got in, Recker opened the door to the passenger side, hopping in beside him.

Surprised, Eldridge wondered what the guy was up to. "What the hell you doing?"

"We're gonna have a little chat," Recker said, calmly leaning over and taking the keys out of the ignition.

"Who are you?"

"Just call me a concerned third party."

"Get the hell out of my car!"

"Now that's no way to get acquainted."

"Dude, get out of my car! If you don't..."

"Then what?" Recker asked. "You'll beat me up? Like you beat up Mia?"

Eldridge was taken aback. "What? You know Mia? How do you know Mia? She send you here?"

"She doesn't know I'm here."

"What're you? Her new boyfriend or something? Is that why she won't see me or return my calls or messages?"

"She won't return your messages because she's afraid of you and that you might beat her up again."

"I've never laid a hand on her," Eldridge said it again.

"Oh, stop. Let's not play games here."

"What do you want?"

"I want you to leave Mia alone. She's done with you. You need to accept that and move on." Recker held Eldridge's gaze.

"Yeah, well, I love her. And she loves me. We're just having a rough patch right now. We'll get through this."

Recker rolled his eyes, knowing this talk was going nowhere. "Listen, idiot. She doesn't love you. She doesn't want anything to do with you. And if you don't move on, and I find out that you're still threatening her, you're gonna find yourself in a lot of trouble."

"Oh yeah? With who?"

Recker stared at him with his menacing eyes. "With me," he said, clenching his jaw. "Keep it up and you're gonna wind up with another visit from me. And I guarantee our next one won't be so chummy."

"Are you done?"

"No. I'm giving you two options. Leave her alone... or wind up in the hospital." Recker then smiled. "I kind of hope you pick the second." Recker tossed back the keys.

He got out of the car and walked back to his own, Eldridge peeling out of the street, leaving tire marks and smoke in his wake. Recker started driving back to the office but got Jones on his com device.

"Jones, just got done having a chat with our friend, Eldridge."

"And how did it go?" Jones asked.

"Tough to say but I don't think he got the message. I'm pretty sure we're gonna have to deal with him again."

"I had a feeling that would be the case. I don't get why she doesn't just contact the police and have him arrested. Surely the text messages and phone calls are a violation of the restraining order."

"That's why it's a worthless piece of paper. It does nothing to protect the victim. Doesn't stop the perpetrator from showing up and a lot of times the victim's afraid to go further. It's only a six-month to a year stay in jail for a restraining order violation. Some women, certainly not all, but some feel that if they send the guy away, he'll come back madder than ever and hurt them even worse than before."

"Well we can't let that happen," Jones said.

"We won't."

"Where are you heading now?"

"Back to the office, I guess."

"Maybe it'd be wiser for you to head to the hospital where Mia works to keep an eye on her."

"Think Eldridge is going there?" Recker checked his rearview mirror. After so many years it was like a tic now.

"Possible. I don't know for sure but I don't think we can adequately protect her from a distance. I think you need to have eyes on her at all times from now on."

"I'm on my way."

Recker drove to St. Mary's Hospital and parked in the lot. Jones had told him that her shift ended at seven, so he had some time to wait. He kept his eyes open just in case Eldridge showed up though he saw no indication yet that he was there. After a half hour of patiently waiting, Recker attentively sat up straight, noticing Eldridge's brown Chevy pickup roll into the parking lot.

"Jones, I just saw Eldridge's pickup come into the parking lot."

"Uh oh. Any sign of Ms. Hendricks yet?"

"Not that I see."

"She should still have at least thirty minutes left on her shift. He might be waiting as well."

"No doubt."

"Do you need assistance?" Jones asked.

"I got it."

Recker kept an eye on the brown pickup as it coasted through the parking lot looking for a spot. Once the truck settled into a spot, Eldridge sat there, apparently doing the same as Recker... waiting. He had parked in a spot that Recker could keep an eye on, so he didn't have to change positions or get out of his car. After about twenty minutes, Eldridge got out of his car and walked toward the entrance of the hospital, waiting in front of a brick wall, out of sight from the entrance doors. Half an hour later, twenty minutes past when her shift was supposed to be over, Hendricks walked out. As soon as she got near the edge of the brick wall, Eldridge stuck his hand out and grabbed her arm, pulling her over to him.

"Let go of me!" she yelled.

Eldridge did let go of her and put his hands up, letting her know he wasn't going to hurt her. "I'm sorry. I'm sorry. I just wanna talk."

"All the talking's over."

"You won't return any of my calls or texts." He shrugged. "I don't know what else to do."

"There's nothing else you can do. We're done."

"C'mon, Mia. You don't mean that."

"I absolutely mean that," Hendricks said, looking around nervously, trying to keep her voice down so nobody else would hear them.

"I just wanna make things right with us. Why won't you give me another chance?"

"I gave you another chance, remember? You blew that one too. And the third one."

Eldridge sighed, looking away from her. "I'm different now."

"Oh really?" she said, "I don't believe you."

"I haven't had a drink in a couple of weeks."

"Good." She nodded. "Maybe another girl will find that appealing."

"I don't want another girl. I want you."

"That's not happening anymore. Ever."

Eldridge was starting to get frustrated at his lack of progress. "Is it that other guy? Is that why you won't give me another chance?"

Hendricks shook her head and shrugged. "What other guy? There is no other guy."

"The one in the trench coat. He paid me a visit today and told me to stay away from you," he told her, sounding a little angrier.

"I don't know what you're talking about. There's no other guy."

"So, you're just gonna lie to my face like that?"

Frustrated herself, Hendricks was also starting to lose her cool. "I don't know what to tell you, Stephen. There is no other guy. I don't know who you talked to today. I don't even know what you're talking about. The reason we're not together anymore is you. And that's never gonna change so please leave me alone. No more texts, no more calls, no more anything."

Eldridge grabbed her arm again, squeezing it tightly. That was a big enough sign for Recker that he needed to move in. He got out of his car and started running for them.

"Stop it! You're hurting me!" Hendricks yelled before breaking free of her ex's grasp.

"I'm sorry... I'm sorry," he told her, wanting to move closer and hug her, but then stepping back.

As soon as Recker stepped on the sidewalk, Eldridge noticed him coming closer.

"There a problem here?" Recker shouted.

With him still remembering Recker's threat from earlier, he completely forgot about Hendricks and kept his eyes fixed on the stranger walking toward him. Thankful that someone was coming, and with Eldridge's concentration elsewhere, Hendricks turned and jogged over to her car. She immediately drove out of the parking lot, not looking back at what was happening behind her.

"You again," Eldridge said.

"I think I warned you already about what would happen if you didn't leave her alone."

"I'm not afraid of you."

"Probably should be," Recker grinned.

Eldridge took a swing at him. Recker ducked the blow, countering with a shot to the left cheek. Eldridge tried another punch. Recker blocked it, countering with a short left to the bridge of Eldridge's nose, blood appearing from a small cut. Eldridge, though stunned and wobbly, tried one more time, this time successfully getting through Recker's defenses, punching him in the side of the stomach. Right near the scar from where he got shot, Recker grimaced in pain, still not a hundred percent healed from the injury. Not wanting to continue the fight any longer, Recker put all of his might into his next shot, punching Eldridge in the face as hard as he could. Eldridge was knocked to the ground, another cut opening up just above his eye. He put his arms down as if he was trying to push himself up but he just couldn't do it. He didn't have the strength. A couple of onlookers rushed over, but still stayed a healthy distance away, not quite sure what to make of the tough-looking stranger standing over the fallen man.

"Think he must've slipped or something," Recker said, moving between the crowd.

Recker went back to his truck and drove away, letting Jones know what happened as he drove. He immediately went to Hendricks' apartment to stake it out in case Eldridge was stupid enough to eventually make his way over there.

Recker had been tailing Hendricks for the last three days. He followed her to work, back to her apartment, to the grocery store, even to the gas station. Not a single sign of Eldridge. According to Jones, Hendricks hadn't received any communication from her ex-boyfriend in the three days since Recker had worked him over. Though Jones was hopeful that his encounter with Recker had finally helped Eldridge wise up, Recker was skeptical that it made much of a difference. In his experience, very few people changed who they were or how they behaved. He expected that he'd run into him soon enough.

It was just after nine o'clock, and Recker followed Hendricks to a large two-story bar that also doubled as a nightclub on the second floor on the weekends. A couple of her friends from the hospital had invited her, and even though that really wasn't her type of scene, she reluctantly agreed to go, hoping it might clear her mind somewhat.

Recker followed her into the bar, making sure he kept some distance from her. He stayed near the end of the room as Hendricks and her friends sat at a table in the corner, sipping on a drink slowly as he kept his eyes on them. The trio of women kept to themselves for the next couple of hours, talking and laughing the night away, though they did rebuff the advances of a few guys who tried hitting on them. Ten minutes after eleven, Recker noticed a very attractive woman, dressed in a short skirt, walk out the front door. Coincidentally, three athletic looking guys who appeared to be in their mid-twenties followed her out the door. Recker thought that he had just assumed the worst of people, but he found it a little too convenient for his tastes. Seeing as how he still hadn't seen Eldridge anywhere, he decided to follow the others out the door.

Recker hadn't stepped outside for more than a few seconds when he heard a woman screaming from the side alley of the bar. There was a small parking area there, only enough for about ten cars lined up against the side of the building. Recker rushed around the corner and saw two of the guys trying to force themselves on the woman while the other stood there as a lookout. Recker ran over to them, the lookout yelling something at him, then started swinging. Recker blocked the punch, then gave him a shot in the kidneys, making the preppy looking guy hunch over. Recker forcefully kneed him in the face, then punched him as he laid on the ground holding his broken nose. He then raced over to the two guys and pulled them both off the girl, ducking one of their blows. Recker took the back of the head of the first guy and drove his head through the passenger side window of the car next to them, half of his body sticking out of the car. The other guy stood there in shock before getting the courage to throw a weak-looking punch that Recker easily side-stepped. Recker gave him a left cross, flooring the man without too much effort. Recker looked back at the woman, still standing by back of the car, stunned by everything that just transpired.

"You OK?" Recker asked, walking over to her.

"Uh, yeah, yeah, I'm OK," she replied. "Thank you so much," she said, giving him a hug. "Are you a cop or something?"

"No. Go inside and tell the bartender what just happened and to call the police."

The woman did as she was instructed and went inside. The first guy that Recker decked started to move around like he was going to get up but Recker gave him a good, solid kick that put him down permanently. Knowing he couldn't stay there too much longer to be questioned with the police on the way, he went back to his truck and just sat there, waiting for Hendricks and her friends to leave the bar. Quite a few people started coming outside to look at the carnage after the woman told her story to the people that worked there and to make sure that the three men didn't go anywhere before the police arrived. Hendricks and her friends came out with the rest of the crowd but didn't stick around much longer. They each got in their separate cars and went their own way, with Recker following Hendricks. She went straight home and appeared to go to bed as Recker waited outside her apartment for another hour to make sure nothing happened.

The following morning, Recker walked into the office, breakfast in hand. Coffee for both of them along with bacon, egg, and cheese sandwiches on a croissant. Just the way he noticed that Jones liked it. With his trained eye, he noticed that Jones had one several days in the past week. Jones was sitting at the desk and working on a computer, not paying much attention to his partner. Recker walked over to him and set the coffee and sandwich on the desk, next to the keyboard.

Jones was a little surprised at the breakfast offering. "What's this?"

"What's it look like? Breakfast," Recker said.

"Yes, I can see that. I mean, at the risk of sounding ungrateful, I don't recall asking you to bring me anything."

"Well, being the sharp fellow that I am, I noticed that you had one of those three days this week. Figured you liked them. Coffee... milk, no sugar."

"While I do appreciate the kind gesture, you must've missed the pattern," Jones said in his usual measured tones.

"What pattern?"

"I try to stick to Monday, Wednesday, Friday for them and filter in other breakfast items on the other days."

"Oh. Sorry about that," Recker said, picking the sandwich back up.

"What're you doing?"

"Well, since today's Saturday, and not a croissant day... I figured I'd eat it for you."

Jones playfully slapped his hand and took the sandwich back. "Since you already took the trouble of getting me one, I suppose I could at least do you the favor of consuming it."

"Kind of a weird thing you got going on there, Jones."

"Yes, well, I suppose we all have our little quirks, don't we?"

Recker took a seat next to him as they ate breakfast together.

"See the morning papers?" Jones said, laying them out in front of Recker.

"No. Not yet."

"It seems that you've made them."

"Me?"

"It would appear that your escapade of helping that young woman at the bar was newsworthy. Story in the Inquirer read, 'Mysterious man in trench coat saves woman from getting raped'."

Recker just listened as he sipped on his coffee.

"Daily News says, 'Woman saved from rapists by trench coat man'. Publicity we could do without, Mr. Recker."

"Well, you hired me to save people. I saw a woman in trouble and I helped."

"Don't misunderstand me, I wasn't criticizing you. You obviously did what you had to do to save that girl. Without you, she almost certainly would've been raped. I just wish it didn't make headlines."

"Well, it's most likely just to be the first. If we're successful in this, we're probably gonna make a lot more.

73

A couple of people out there in the city saving people from bad guys, who aren't law enforcement... is bound to make headlines. That's a big news story," Recker said, trying to see what Jones' point was.

"Perhaps. And perhaps it wouldn't have been if one of the perpetrators hadn't had his head thrown through a car window."

Recker opened his mouth to say something, then closed it as he thought about what Jones just said. "Did you just criticize me?"

"Not at all. Just openly wondering if there could've been another way the situation could've been handled other than... so violently."

"Jones, when you're in a fight against three men at one time, you don't worry about anything other than disabling them as soon as possible. Whatever way is necessary. I don't think talking them to death was much of an option."

"As I said, Mr. Recker, you're probably completely right in how you handled it."

They stayed sitting there, eating their breakfast and drinking their coffee, browsing through the newspapers. Recker figured he'd try to get to know Jones a little better. His employer seemed to know quite a bit about him, but Recker knew very little the other way around. All he knew was that Jones once worked for the NSA.

"So, why'd you pick this city?" Recker said.

Jones picked his head up from reading the paper and looked at him quizzically. "I don't follow your question."

"Well you're not from around here so I was just wondering what made you settle here."

"What makes you believe that I wasn't born here?"

"Because you're obviously too smart for that. Anyone intelligent enough to work for the NSA, smart enough to create new identities for himself and others, and crafty enough to hack into government files and databases, as well as banks of criminals and filter money into a secret account... isn't dumb enough to go back to the city he was born in, or for that matter, any city which he was ever associated with prior to this," Recker said.

Jones grinned, though not surprised that Recker would come to that conclusion. He would've been disappointed in his abilities if he didn't. "Very astute deductions, Mr. Recker. You are correct. I've been here approximately two months, and before that, never stepped foot in this city before."

"So... why here?"

Jones shrugged. "I don't know. I guess I figured it was a large enough city to blend in and... large enough that it had plenty of problems and issues where we could help and make a difference."

"So where are you from originally?"

Jones took a deep breath, unsure if he wanted to divulge any more information. Recker tried to set his mind at ease, knowing they had to trust each other if the partnership was to work and be effective.

"If you want me to go on with us, then I need to be sure I can trust you," Recker said.

"Why would you not trust me already? I've told you I worked for the NSA. I told you I diverted your flight from Florida, where Centurion agents were surely waiting for you to finish what they started in London. I believe I saved your life, whether you wanted me to or not. I've given you employment. What else can I do to gain your trust?"

"You can start by telling me who you really are. What you're about?"

"I've already done that."

"No. No, you haven't. You've told me what you want to accomplish and how you acquire the information that you do. But you haven't told me who you are."

Jones just looked at Recker for several moments. "I guess it's just... I just fail to see why that's important."

"How am I supposed to trust somebody that I don't really know? Something comes up on that screen of yours and I'm supposed to follow it without asking questions?"

"So when you worked for the CIA, you knew exactly everything and didn't work in the shadows with only snippets of information?" Jones said.

"This isn't the CIA. Or the NSA, for that matter. I knew I was working for the government and I'd be doing highly questionable things that I had no clue the reasoning behind. That didn't end so well for me and I'm not about to make that mistake again. If I work for someone, anyone, then I need to know all the facts. No more games, no more guesses, no more secrets."

"That is a two-way street, Mr. Recker. I could say the same thing for you."

Recker's head snapped back, unsure what he was talking about. "How's that?"

"Well, I know quite a bit about you already. But there is one thing that has been puzzling me though."

"What's that?"

"You were ambushed in London. Nearly killed. But you survived and spent six months in hiding."

"What's so strange about that?"

"That you used a known alias to book a flight to Orlando, surely knowing that alias would pop up on the CIA's radar."

"You already figured that out. I wasn't planning on leaving that airport."

"So, you were planning on going down in a blaze of glory?" Jones' eyebrows raised.

"Sure."

"No. No, I don't think so. I don't believe that a man who survives an attack and nearly dies, then hides out for six months, suddenly plans on going down in a hail of gunfire. If that were the case, you would've decided to do that days, if not minutes, after getting out of the hospital. Or you never would've gone to the hospital to begin with. Your reasoning for doing so eludes me, but you had a reason for choosing Orlando. I just haven't figured it out yet. Of course, if you'd like to share, then perhaps... perhaps we both can divulge some of our inner secrets."

Recker thought about it for a minute, staring ahead but not looking at anything. He really hadn't planned on spilling the beans on why he was really going to Orlando, but he figured that if he did, maybe Jones could actually be useful in helping him track down the man he was looking for. If Jones could find him, he should be able to find Agent Seventeen. Eventually, he knew he'd have to turn to someone for help. Since he didn't know if he could trust any of his former contacts, he'd have to find someone who was on the outside. Maybe Jones was that guy.

"OK," Recker said, finally making up his mind. "You're right. I wasn't planning on going there just to meet my maker. I was looking for someone."

"But you had to know Centurion would be there waiting."

"I was counting on it."

"It's still not making much sense yet. Who exactly were you looking for there?"

"One agent."

"Who?"

"I don't know his name. I only know his codename. Agent Seventeen."

"Is he a friend?"

"Hardly. I've never met him. But when I do... I will kill him," Recker said.

"Why would you want to kill someone you've never met? Do you think he's the one responsible for what happened in London?"

"No." Recker shook his head. "He's just a regular operative... like me. You know, I'm not even angry about what happened in London. It's a secret world full of people in the shadows. You kill, people try to kill you, and it goes around and round. When you live in that world, you learn to expect things like that."

"I'm still not connecting the dots," Jones said, his eyebrows now furrowed.

Recker's eyes became glossy as he thought about

Carrie and what happened to her. "I made the... uh... unfortunate mistake of meeting a woman."

Jones could tell by Recker's manner of speaking that it was uncomfortable for him. He seemed to be deeply moved and there was an intensity in his eyes that seemed to consume him.

"And I fell in love with her," Recker said, the words starting to tumble out. "And she had the misfortune of falling in love with me."

"So, that's who you were going to Orlando to see?" Jones paused for a moment, getting the picture straight in his head. "None of that information was in any of your records."

"Usually isn't."

"So, what does this Agent Seventeen have to do with her?"

Recker clenched his jaws as he described what happened. "He killed her."

Jones closed his eyes, having a feeling that's where he was heading with the story. "I'm very sorry for your loss."

"So am I."

"What happened? When did it happen?"

"The night I was attacked in London. They came for her too."

"Why? What harm could she be?"

"No loose ends. If they got rid of me, they couldn't risk her living to tell anything that I might have told her in confidence. After I killed the two agents sent to kill me, as I walked to the hospital, I called her just to make sure she was all right. A man answered the phone. He told me he killed her."

"How do you know it was this Agent Seventeen?"

"He told me his codename. It was like he was taunting me, not expecting me to live the night. He probably assumed the attack on me wouldn't fail and I'd never live long enough to remember his name," Recker was gripping the edge of his desk.

"Are you sure she's dead? Maybe he was only telling you that to provoke you for some reason. It wouldn't be the first time that..."

"She's dead," Recker said, releasing his grip and holding one hand up. "While I was recovering in London, I searched online for any news that I could find on her. And I found it. Her obituary. They covered it up by making it look like a house fire. Carrie Brodin, twenty-nine years old, the only victim in a fire that engulfed her home, burned it down to the ground." Recker could vividly remember every word of the article.

"Carrie, she was why you'd grown weary of the agency, wasn't it?"

Recker nodded. "I never expected to meet someone like her. After I left the agency, another year or so... I probably would've asked her to marry me."

"Was she aware of what you did?"

"Not at first. I kept it from her to protect her. And probably because I was sure she'd want nothing to do with me if she did know. But, after a while, once things got more serious, I told her. I expected that'd be the end of us. That she wouldn't want me anymore."

"But that wasn't the case?"

"No. I think it might've made her love me even more. The hardened killer whose heart she softened. I think she found me a challenge. She always liked a good challenge." Recker smiled.

"So, what was your intention in Orlando?"

"To kill whatever Centurion agents came looking for me and get the information I needed. Unless Seventeen was one of them."

"You mean, you were just going to keep killing agents until you found the one you were looking for?"

"That was the plan."

"While I sympathize with your loss, Mr. Recker, you can't just keep killing whoever's unlucky enough to be in your path until you find the one person that you're looking for," Jones said.

Recker shrugged. "Seemed like a good enough plan at the time."

"Well if that was your plan then why did you agree to my offer?"

"I'm not sure exactly. I guess it just struck a nerve."

"I don't know if I believe that. You don't strike me as the type who does things on impulse. You're usually already thinking several steps ahead."

"Well, it certainly wasn't what I was thinking when I agreed to this little enterprise of yours, but now? Now I'm thinking maybe you can help me."

It didn't take Jones long to realize what Recker was implying. He knew what he wanted. "You mean you want me to help you locate this Agent Seventeen."

Recker made a face and shrugged, which was as much of an acknowledgment as Jones was getting. "It occurred to me."

"What makes you think I can find this... mysterious agent?"

"You found me. You can find him," Recker said.

"So, what you're asking, is to help you find this man so you can execute him?"

Recker nodded. "If that's how you want to interpret it. I look at it as finding the man who executed the woman I loved."

"I'm not sure I can do that." Jones rubbed his eyes. "To have someone's death directly tied to my hands, albeit one of questionable character, is not something I'm sure I want to be a part of."

Recker looked a little disappointed, but certainly wasn't going to beg for help. "That's your call. But know this... I'm going to look for him on my own, and when I find him, I'm gonna leave you and this place the moment that I do."

"And if you do, when that happens, even if it's a year from now, you'd risk leaving behind and throwing away everything we might have built up?" Jones said, becoming more animated.

"Listen, this is your project, not mine. If you were to help me, maybe I could be persuaded to stick around when I was done with him."

"Assuming you'd come back from whatever predicament you were running into."

"I'm gonna do what I have to do. The rest is your call."

Recker stood up and walked around the room for a few minutes, finally stopping by the one window in the room, overlooking the laundromat. He watched a few cars pull out of the lot and onto the main road. Jones watched his newfound companion as he gazed out the window, thinking about their predicament. After about five minutes, Jones finally broke the silence.

"If I were to agree to this plan of yours, I can't guarantee a specific time frame of finding this man. It could take weeks, it could take months."

"That's OK. My hatred will still burn no matter how long it takes," Recker said, turning back around to the desk area to face his partner. "How exactly did you find me?"

"I had stumbled across your situation during some of my... well, let's just say, some of the files I happened to come across."

"So how did you know where I was when Centurion didn't?"

"I didn't. I wrote down a list of several agents who were of interest to me. Yours happened to be one of them. I left the NSA about a month after your situation in London. I spent the next three months looking for you, not physically, but on the internet with any crumbs of information I could find on you. But I couldn't turn up a thing."

"Yeah, it was a pretty good spot I found," Recker said, walking around the desk.

"So I put you, and all of your aliases on my watch list. Two months later, John Smith popped up as buying a plane ticket to Orlando. I thought you'd made a grave error in deciding to use a known alias and used a rather clever hack to change the plane's destination. So, whoever was waiting for you, believes that you actually got off the plane in Virginia, then rented a car to St. Louis. From there you went on to Texas."

"I was wondering about that. About why they wouldn't see that I came to Philadelphia."

"Little did I know that it wasn't a mistake on your part. If I'd known it was intentional, well, maybe we wouldn't be having this conversation today."

"If you're feeling a little too uncomfortable with my situation, Jones, feel free to hire somebody else. I won't think bad of you for it. And I give you my word I'll never say a word about this to anyone else," Recker said.

Jones gave a half smile. "Thank you, Mr. Recker, but that won't be necessary. And though I believe you in that you would keep all this quiet, I don't feel the need to hire anyone other than you. You see, I do trust you. I do believe I hired the right person for this. So if I want you to help me... then I need to help you."

Recker sat back down on one of the chairs by the computers. He spilled his guts, let his heart down on his sleeve and revealed his innermost feelings to Jones, just as he'd wanted. Now, it was Jones' turn to reveal his.

"So, now that you know what my true endgame was and is out on the table, why don't you do the same?" Recker said.

Jones squinted at him and nodded, agreeing. "You are correct in that my motivations, though honorable, are not completely just about saving humankind. Much like yourself, I've had to deal with a personal loss, which is a big reason why I'm here today."

"What happened?"

Though Jones was still a bit hesitant to divulge information about himself, he knew he had to in order to further gain Recker's trust. "You're right. I'm not from Philadelphia, or even this state. I'm originally from Chicago. Well, a suburb just outside of Chicago. As for my real name, that's something you'll never know. As far as I'm concerned, the person I was before is dead. He will never return. Much like you're now known as Michael Recker, for me, from now on, my name will only ever be David Jones."

"So what got you into this?"

"Though I obviously knew and was aware of the NSA's ability to filter information from multiple sources from everyday people, I never really thought much about the consequences, or lack thereof the same. They do a very good job of identifying and tagging people who are a national security threat."

"But?"

"But the amount of information they receive that they just let slip through their fingers that could help regular, normal people is staggering. I believe we've already discussed the reasons why, and they're valid, but I just couldn't keep watching good, valuable intelligence be thrown away."

"What happened to change your mind?" Recker said, swiveling in his chair to face his partner.

"My brother. He died last year in a robbery," Jones said,

remembering the event like it was yesterday. "He owned a bar. One night, he was closing up, just him and one of his employees. As they walked out the door, they were both shot and killed."

"I'm sorry to hear it."

"The men who did it were caught and apprehended rather quickly. But several months later, I read something about how the men sent texts to each other about the robbery before it happened, planning it. So I went back into some of the NSA archives, found their names and phone numbers, and there it was. The NSA had data that the bar my brother owned was going to be robbed by these men." Jones shrugged his shoulders. "And they did nothing. It didn't pertain to national security, so it didn't really matter in their eyes." Jones' eyes flicked back to his screen for a moment, then back to meet Recker's gaze.

"That's pretty rough."

Jones sighed as he continued. "So, it was then that I decided I needed to break free of the NSA and branch out on my own. I wanted to help others and try to prevent something like what happened to my brother. I spent the next several months working on a program that sends the information the NSA gets to my own personal servers. Then I figured out how the rest... how to finance this operation, how to operate, where to go."

"And who to hire."

"I have many skills, but I lack certain traits. Those are the traits that you have."

"How is it possible to grab the information from the

NSA without them knowing it?" Recker said, his eyebrows screwed up emphasizing his question.

"It's a very complex formula of which I'll spare you the technical details. Suffice to say that the NSA receives such huge packets of data, and once it's logged into their servers, that even if the smallest amount was diverted to me, they'd be alerted."

"So how do you do it?"

"I developed a program that takes a very small amount of data, only from this area, copies and redirects the copy to my computers at the very same time as it's uploaded to the NSA's servers."

"So they're not aware of it being taken from them?"

"Correct, because as far as they're concerned, nothing is missing," Jones said, leaning back on his chair, hands behind his head. "They're still getting the data that they're supposed to be getting. I'm just pilfering a small amount of it and concealing the whereabouts." He smiled a self-satisfied smile at his achievement.

Recker hoped that Jones was as good as he seemed to be but he still had questions. "What if they did some type of system check and noticed the data being redirected?"

"In that event, they would find the information going to a server in Washington... the state, not D.C. Further investigation would find them following the trail from there to Texas, to North Dakota, to Maine, and so on and so on, even with a couple of stops in Canada and Europe thrown in for good measure."

"How are you able to do that?"

"As I said, I'll spare you the technical details. Unless

you have years of programming knowledge, it's unlikely you'd understand anything I told you. Just understand that what I've done is not really supposed to be possible." Jones was shaking his head slightly.

"So how is it that you were able to find me?" Recker said.

"The NSA has tools that make it possible to also lift the layers of other United States government agencies' private and secure files. While I was still there, though on the verge of leaving, I thought it might be a good idea to look at potential candidates who I thought could help me on my endeavor."

"Who had my experience?"

"I was, in particular, looking at certain agencies who specialized in clandestine operations and were experts at multiple activities. In addition, I was looking for people who had at least five years of experience, and in my view... limited time left at their then current location."

Jones turned back to his screen and clattered at his keyboard seemingly finished with his story but it occurred to Recker that Jones might already have the name of Agent Seventeen when he was initially searching through the CIA's records. "Do you have those records or files from when you found me? Maybe the guy I'm looking for is in there."

"I'm afraid not," Jones said, shaking his head. "All I have left are the files and information from the final five agents I was considering."

Recker sighed, figuring it was just his luck that Jones

didn't already have the information he was looking for. "Figures."

"I'm sorry. I didn't think I'd need it. I didn't think I'd ever have use for all of that information anymore. Besides, the man you're looking for might not even have been in my search, anyway."

"Possible."

"Might not have been on the job for the five-year requirement I was looking for," Jones said.

"Maybe." Recker rubbed his clean-shaven chin prompting a burst of the smell of his aftershave to waft gently over him. "How soon can you start looking for him?"

"I can start within the next couple of days. It could take some time, though. First, I no longer have the NSA program that hacks into the CIA database. So that means I'll have to create my own. That will take time to make sure that it's invisible to them, or in the event they notice, leads them on a wild goose chase to Timbuktu."

"I understand. I know one thing though, no matter how long it takes…" Recker said, his voice trailing off.

"Yes?"

"He's on borrowed time."

6

The following morning, Jones was already in the office by eight, as seemed to be his trademark. Recker came in a few minutes after eight to get instructions for the day. As soon as he walked in, his phone started ringing. Considering he hadn't been in town very long, and he only had two phone numbers programmed into his phone, one of them being in the same room with him, he knew who it was before even looking at it. Unless it was a wrong number. It wasn't.

"What can I do for you, Tyrell?" Recker said into his phone.

"I wanted to meet up with you for a few minutes if you got the time."

"Why? Did you acquire those other items on my wish list yet?"

"Nah, not yet. That'll prolly take a little time. There's a couple of other things I wanted to talk about."

"Such as?"

"Rather do it in person. One thing I've learned over the years is not to discuss business over the phone. Never know who's listening," Gibson said. From what Jones had told him, Recker knew very well.

"All right. Time and place."

"Art museum. Make it an hour."

"I'll be there," Recker said, ending the conversation.

"Who was that?" Jones said.

"That was our friend, Tyrell."

"You have a curious opinion on what constitutes a friend."

"Can't all be peace lovers and churchgoers."

"I suppose not. What was it about?"

"Oh, he wants to meet up for some reason."

"Has he located the rest of your merchandise?"

"Says no," Recker said, looking at the wall trying to figure out what he might want.

"You don't suppose it's a trap of some sort, do you?"

"I doubt they'd set a trap at the art museum."

"The art museum?" Jones thought about that for a few seconds. "Yes, you're probably right."

Recker went over to the new steel gun cabinet that adorned the far wall by the corner. He took out two of the pistols, a Glock and a Sig, and put them in their respective holsters, one in the back of his pants and one on his left side.

"Do you really think you'll need both of them for some reason?" Jones said, peering up at him over his laptop.

"Never know. Always have to be prepared. Just in case."

Recker smiled back at the slightly worried look on Jones' face.

"Well, I understand that, but why are you taking two?"

"Always carry a backup weapon," Recker said, he felt like he was an instructor on a rookie agent's first day. It wasn't far off the truth. "Just in case something happens to the first one. Misfire, lost, stolen, taken… whatever the case may be."

"You certainly are thorough."

"You know, I was thinking, how exactly did you go about finding Ms. Hendricks? Or anybody else for that matter?"

"I thought we already discussed all that?"

"No, you told me the process for how you get the information. You didn't exactly say how you get a name. I mean, she must not be the only name in that little system of yours."

Jones felt like he was an instructor on some green computer geek's first day as a spook. That wasn't far off the truth either. "Well the names don't just fall out of the sky, Mr. Recker. I actually have to do some work to identify the potential victim. This isn't like a TV show or something. I don't just get a name or a number and hand it over to you. I get snippets of information I already told you about then I go to work. I cross reference the code phrases that alarmed the system and match them up against phone numbers, emails and such, then try to get the names of the particular parties involved and assess the threat levels, figuring out who exactly is in need of our assistance. It can be quite involved and doesn't happen in a matter of minutes."

Recker raised his eyebrows. "Sounds reasonable to me. I was just wondering." It actually sounded deadly dull. Give him some jerk to deal with and he was happy. Fiddling around with data felt as if it would be like a slow day in hell to him.

"And no, Ms. Hendricks is not the only victim on our radar. She just so happens to be first on our radar. The others will be coming shortly."

Recker smiled and nodded. "I'll catch up with you later." He was glad to be out of there for now.

Recker walked out of the office and down the wooden steps. He stood there for a moment and pulled out his phone, contemplating dialing a number, the one person on the planet he knew he could trust. Although he believed everything Jones had told him to that point, after everything that had happened to him, trust wasn't something that came easy for Recker. His gut told him that everything Jones had said was honest and accurate, but if Recker was to keep on going with this arrangement, he needed to be a hundred percent sure that his new partner was completely trustworthy. Recker walked around the building to the parking lot and started to punch in the number he knew by memory.

"Hello? Who's this?" A man's voice.

"Alpha Two One Seven, Delta Six Four Three," Recker said on autopilot.

"Oh, it's you. Didn't recognize the phone number."

"Well, considering everything that's happened, I figure I'll need to change them every few months."

"How are you holding up?"

"Pretty good. All the injuries have basically healed."

"Where you at these days?"

"Cleveland." Recker lied without the slightest hesitation.

"How's the weather there?"

"Harsh."

"I know you didn't call to chat about the weather," the man said. "What's up?"

"I need a favor."

"Another one? Already? After what I did for you in London?"

"You owed me that one in London," Recker said.

The voice hesitated for a moment. "Yeah, I did. What do you need?"

"Information."

"What kind?"

"The kind you can't get from a simple internet search through the white pages."

"You don't say." The voice chuckled.

"I need anything you can dig up on any NSA agents, consultants, anyone that has left the agency over the past eight months or so."

"Looking for anything in particular?"

"Yeah. If you see one from the Chicago area, that's the one I'm interested in," Recker said as he started to walk toward his truck.

"What's the connection?"

"He might be able to help me in finding Agent Seventeen."

"I see six months hasn't changed your appetite for that."

"Never."

"I'll call you in a couple of days with anything I come up with," the man said then hung up.

Recker got in his truck and drove down to the art museum, one of Philadelphia's biggest tourist attractions. He parked on nearby Pennsylvania Avenue and walked over to the building. The museum was famous for its steps. Used in the movie Rocky when the character ran up them, many visitors tried doing the same. Recker, not being Rocky or a tourist and not seeing Gibson at the bottom of the steps, walked up to see if he was waiting by the entrance. He looked around for a few minutes but still didn't see him. He went back down about halfway then sat down on a ledge on the outer edge of the steps. About five minutes later, he noticed Gibson walking toward him.

"Few minutes late," Recker told him.

"Traffic."

"So what's up?" Recker asked, watching people walk past.

"Jeremiah asked me to meet up with you."

"What for? He got my other merchandise?"

"Nah, man, it's not like that," Gibson said, looking around constantly. "He's a little... worried about you."

"Why?"

Gibson dropped his voice as a couple of tourists ran past them, cameras swinging. "Cause you're new, and a wildcard. You come in like some sort of badass buying guns, looking like you're James Bond or something."

"I'm an unknown."

"Yeah. He wants to know what you're up to and whose side you're on."

"I told you already. What I'm up to is my business. Whose side I'm on would depend on who we're talking about," Recker said.

"Men like you don't just pop up out of the blue usually, unless you were brought in by somebody."

"And Jeremiah thinks I'm here to start some type of turf war or something?"

"I think he's more worried about you being here to finish a turf war."

"Well, you can tell Jeremiah that I'm not. I wasn't brought here by anybody and I'm not interested in whatever war he's got going on. I'm not a player in it."

"Then why are you here?" Gibson said. "You obviously got something going on."

The two tourists walked back past them on the way down, trying to laugh and pant at the same time.

"Let's just say I was brought in for security purposes for certain individuals... none of which should be of any concern to Jeremiah."

"I'll let him know."

"That should put his mind at ease a little bit."

"Maybe. He hates new wrinkles though."

"Tell your boss I'm not one of them," Recker said.

"Well, I'll tell him, but he ain't my boss."

"Then why are you here?"

"He asked me to talk to you. Figured you'd be more willing to talk to me than someone in his crew that you don't know."

"Makes sense. If you don't work for him, how come you always seem to be around him?"

"I didn't say I didn't work for him. I do some jobs for him here and there but I ain't part of the crew. I'm my own guy, do my own thing, sometimes I'll do something for him if I need some bread real quick."

"Well if you're not part of his crew, then maybe you can explain a few things for me."

"Depends," Gibson said.

"Tell me what all this stuff Jeremiah's worried about is."

Gibson scouted all round to make sure nobody was listening in.

"I'll break it down real quick for you. There's three factions fighting for control of this city."

"I take it all of these factions are of the illegal variety."

"Depends on what you mean by illegal, man. There's some cops in this city who are worse than the people they lock up."

Recker laughed. "What about these factions? I take it one of them is Jeremiah?"

"Yeah. Jeremiah runs the north and west side of Philly. Vincent controls the northeast. Then there's the Italians, they run everything downtown," Gibson said, resisting the temptation to swing his arms around pointing in the various directions.

"Who's in charge of the Italians?"

"Man named Marco Bellomi. Man, if you do get mixed up in any of this, stay clear of him."

"Why is that?"

"Violent guy. Quick temper. Not somebody you wanna cross."

"How do you figure in all of this?" Recker said, keeping his eyes fixed on Gibson.

"I don't."

"But you know all the players?"

"Like I said, I'm my own guy. I've done work for Jeremiah. I've even had business with Vincent. I only know of Bellomi by reputation."

"And these guy's trust you? Enemies, fighting against each other, but they both employ the same guy."

"Listen, they both know I ain't spying for nobody, ain't killing nobody, ain't setting nobody up to get killed, nothin' like that. I do small jobs for them but they know they can trust me and I ain't up in their business."

"So, why is that?"

"Why you wanting to know?"

"You asked me a bunch of questions. Figured it was my turn. I've seen your file, no major arrests."

"How'd you get my file?" Gibson said, turning to look directly at Recker with a surprised look on his face. "If you ain't a cop, how'd you get that?"

Recker smiled. "I have my little ways. Listen, if I feel I can trust you, I may have some work for you in the future."

"If you mean snitchin' on anybody, that won't fly. I ain't no snitch, man."

"Good. Don't need one. Cops use snitches. Since I'm

not a cop, I got no use for one. I'm just talking if I ever need some information, you seem like you're... well connected," Recker said.

"You mean for your... security firm?" Gibson said. He still sounded like he needed some convincing.

Recker looked over at him and smiled. "Yeah."

"I dunno, man. We'll see. Depends on what you're looking for."

"Well, when the time comes, I'll let you know."

They sat for a few minutes, neither saying anything, just watching the people go by and more tourists running up the steps.

Finally, Recker opened up, intrigued by the underworld factions fighting for control of the city.

"Tell me more about this upcoming war, what's behind it?"

"What's any war about? They want what they ain't got, and more of what they do," Gibson said.

"What about the players? Who do you think has the upper hand?"

"That's a tough one, man. I don't even know. They all got their pros and cons if you know what I mean. Bellomi, he's a shoot first, ask questions later type of guy. He don't wait around for trouble to find him. He looks for it first. He even got an inkling of something bein' up, you're knee deep in it."

"What about the others?"

"Jeremiah and Vincent are pretty similar, actually. Smart guys. They sit back. Watch. Observe. Wait for the right opportunity, then strike."

"They're not impulsive."

"Nah. But they ain't weak neither. Don't think they're the kind of guys you wanna cross cause you don't. Not unless you're prepared to eat some lead. They don't go looking for trouble, but they won't back down from it neither."

"They'd rather fly under the radar," Recker said. He understood that strategy.

"Yeah. That Bellomi, though, he's a different type of cat all together. He don't care about nothing. Don't care if you know he did something."

"So how'd you escape getting caught up in it?"

"Whatcha mean?"

"You say you're a solo operator. How come you didn't get recruited into one of their organizations?"

"What, just cause I'm a black man from the streets, you think I gotta be caught up in a gang or something?"

"No, because you do business with all of them. How come none of them tried to put you on the payroll?" Recker said.

"Hey, I only do business with two of them. I don't mess with Bellomi."

"So what's your story?"

"Whad'ya mean?"

"Well, if you're working with all these guys, then they obviously respect you enough to keep you on board. I'm sure they've tried recruiting you at some point. Why not fall in?"

Gibson shifted on the hard ledge, shaking his head. "I like doing my own thing. Don't have to answer to nobody, don't have to follow nobody's orders, just my own."

"And they're OK with that?"

"Like I said, I've built up trust with them. They know I'm not out to screw nobody. Just looking out for me."

"Got a family?"

Gibson hesitated before answering, not sure if he wanted to reveal anything. "Yeah. Got my mom and a little brother."

"How they feel about what you do?"

"Mom worries. But that's what moms do, right?"

Recker smiled. "Yeah. I guess so. What about your brother? He caught up in all this too?"

"Nah. He's only fourteen right now. In ninth grade."

"Let me guess, you're the breadwinner, right?" Recker said.

"Yeah. It's all good though."

"Hopefully your brother doesn't follow your foot-steps... no offense meant."

Gibson laughed. "You're crazy, man, you know that?"

"May have been told that once or twice before."

"Nah, my brother ain't following my footsteps. He's the reason I keep doing this."

"How's that?"

"My brother's smart. Smarter than me. He loves read-ing, loves to learn, likes those graphic novel type books, you know what I mean?"

"Yeah." Recker nodded. He'd seen them on the news-stands but never read one. All that superhero stuff? Not his cup of tea.

"I do what I do so I can get enough money to put him through college so he can make something out of himself, so he's not on the streets, hustling like the rest of us."

"Noble of you."

"Just looking out for my brother. He's too nice for this type of stuff. Don't got the personality for it."

"So how come you never went?"

"Went where?" Gibson said absentmindedly, watching a long-legged blonde with her boyfriend as they walked up the steps toward them.

"College."

"My mom barely had enough money to put food on the table, man. College was nothing but a dream for me. Didn't have good enough grades for scholarships or nothing like that."

"What about a regular job?" Recker eyed the blonde as she passed them by. She reminded him of... Gibson's voice brought him back.

"What? Working at McDonald's? Not for me, man, not for me."

"There's other stuff. Construction, truck driver, warehouse... there's other things."

"I dunno. Maybe. Not an option anymore. I'm already in what I'm in. And I'm gonna make sure my brother has enough money to go to whatever college he wants to go to."

"So that's why you don't get involved in anything heavy?"

"I ain't getting involved in no killin' or robbin' or any of that. My brother ain't going to college if the money ain't there. And it won't be if I'm dead or locked up, y'know what I mean?"

"You seem like a decent guy, Tyrell."

"I dunno about all that. I've done stuff. I'm just looking out for me and my family."

The two sat for a while, shooting the breeze, more at ease with each other as the minutes passed by. Both of them could tell that the other wasn't there under false pretenses or trying to put something over on the other. Just two regular guys having a talk.

"So you gonna tell me what you're really here for?" Gibson asked. "Who you really are?"

"I already did."

Gibson laughed. "Man, you ain't told me nothing. Just ran around the subject a bunch of times."

"Can't tell you any more than I already have. For my protection... and yours."

Gibson leaned back for a second, wondering what he meant by that. He thought he had it figured out though. "You on the run from somebody? Cops?"

Recker smiled, shaking his head. "Maybe someday I'll tell you. For now, all you need to know is that I'm not in law enforcement, I'm not working for criminals, and I'm here to protect people," Recker said. "I'm one of the good guys, that's all you need to know."

They talked for a few minutes more, then went their separate ways.

Recker wanted to check back in on Hendricks. When she was on the night shift, she usually stopped by a diner and had lunch there before going off to work. If he timed it right, he could get there just a few minutes before she did. As he was driving, his phone rang. This time, it was the only other number that was in his phone.

"What's up, Professor?" Recker said with a sarcastic edge.

"Professor? You do realize who this is, right?" Jones replied.

Recker chuckled, "Yes, don't you like your new nickname?"

"I didn't realize I had one."

"You kind of remind me of a professor."

"Are you insulting me?"

"Of course not. I mean it in only the most positive ways and with the utmost respect."

"Hmm. Not sure I believe that."

"You're kind of like a professor. You're smart, seem to have all the answers, you even dress like one."

"Be that as it may, I was just calling to find out about your meeting with Mr. Gibson," Jones said.

"Oh. Went OK."

"What was he after?"

"Seems as though there's a turf war on the verge of happening. Jeremiah's one of the players and wanted to make sure I wasn't going to turn up, gunning for one of the other sides," Recker said.

"Perhaps it would be wise to avoid all the players in this game for a while. I don't think it'd be in our best interests to get mixed up in it."

"Well, I agree about not taking an interest in it, but we may not be able to avoid them altogether."

"Why do you say that?" Jones sounded concerned.

"Well, that depends on where our cases take us, doesn't it?"

"Yes, I suppose you're right."

"Plus, no matter what happens, it's always beneficial to know the players in the game, even if you're not in it."

"Why is that?"

"What they do, at some point, even in a roundabout way, may have some consequence on what we're doing," Recker said. "In any case, I'll stay in contact with Gibson so we have ears on what's going on. Plus, he may be someone we can turn to for information on the street if the need arises."

"It sounds as though you made a new friend. Are you sure you can trust him?"

"Not yet. But I don't think he's a bad guy. He seems like someone who's not interested in hurting or killing people. Just looking out for his family. Wants to send his younger brother to college to get him away from this life."

"Hmm, seems to be an honorable and worthy choice on his part even if he had chosen an unorthodox route."

"Yeah. I'll tell you more about it when I get back to the office. Right now I'm on my way to the diner where Hendricks usually goes before work. I'll tail her for a little bit before she goes in."

Recker arrived at Joe's Diner a little after noon, and was sitting at a window booth near the rear of the establishment. He sat facing the door so he could see Hendricks when she came in. He didn't have much of a wait as she came walking in about ten minutes after he did. As soon as she walked in, Recker put his head down like he was reading the menu so she didn't notice him. It didn't work. She was being shown to her own table when she saw Recker sitting in the corner. Though she didn't get a great look at the guy that intervened at the hospital, she recognized his haircut and coat. She also remembered seeing someone similar at the bar where the woman was attacked.

"Actually, I see someone over there that I know, I'll just sit with him," Hendricks told the waitress.

Recker kept his head down for a few moments until someone sat down across from him. He smelt perfume. Without picking his head up, he raised his eyebrows to see his visitor. Seeing it was Hendricks, he closed his eyes for a second, mad at himself for getting made.

"Hi," Recker said, pretending not to know who she was.

"Hi," she said, flashing a smile. It was a nice smile Recker thought.

"Can I help you with anything?"

"Yes, you can. You can tell me why you're following me for starters."

Recker cleared his throat then coughed as he stalled while he thought of a reason. "I'm not sure what you're talking about, ma'am."

"Is this really how you wanna do this?"

"Do what?" Recker said, pretending not to understand.

"The stupid act doesn't suit you," Hendricks said.

"It doesn't, huh?"

Hendricks shook her head. "No, it doesn't."

Recker grabbed his drink off the table and took a sip of the soda. "So what can I do for you?"

"You can tell me who you are and why you're following me."

"Why would you think I'm following you? I was here before you, remember?"

"Let's see... oh yes, you showed up at the hospital and beat up my ex. I couldn't really see your face too well then, but I noticed the close shaved military haircut and nice trench coat of yours. Then there was some trouble at a bar a couple of days ago where a woman was almost raped. Some guy in a trench coat saved her," she said, tilting her head and looking at his coat. "Kind of like yours."

Recker smiled. "A lot of guys wear trench coats."

"You know, I thought I saw a guy leave the bar a few minutes before that girl was attacked. I didn't quite see his face, again, but his hairstyle reminded me of that guy at the hospital. Kind of like yours."

"I hear this look's all the rage these days." Recker laughed.

"It's a nice look," Hendricks said. "It's uh... quite a coincidence that I find you here, I mean, fitting the description of those other people and all."

"Isn't it?"

Hendricks took her phone out of her purse. "So are you gonna make me do it or are you gonna tell me the truth?"

"Do what?"

"Call the police. If I feel I'm being followed, especially

since I have a restraining order out, I'm very jumpy, I should call the police, don't you think?"

Recker knew she was playing him, trying to bluff him into revealing his true intentions. He could just get up and leave and not say another word, but that seemed like it might be counterproductive at this point. He figured that she knew he was there, and at least had some indication of who he was, or what he was doing. If he just left, and she saw him again at another time, it might lead to the same conversation all over again, or maybe even worse. Also, the fact that she was there and approached him, as well as initiated a conversation with him, meant that she didn't feel threatened by him. That was a plus on his side. After thinking about it, he decided the best course of action was to let her know that he was there to protect her. Maybe that'd even make the job easier for him. If she was in on everything, it would help him if she advised him on everywhere she was going or planned to be.

"Well, what's it gonna be?" Hendricks asked, tapping her thumb on her phone.

"How about if we just leave it at, I'm here to look after you and make sure you're safe?" Recker said, knowing full well that wouldn't satisfy her.

She shook her head. "Who are you?"

"My name's Recker."

"Interesting name."

Recker grinned. "I've heard it before."

"What's your first name?"

"Michael."

"I'd reciprocate but I have the feeling you already know mine."

"Kind of ballsy, coming over here, talking to a stranger who you think is following you."

Hendricks made a face, scrunching her nose. "Not really. You stepped in and took on my ex, you stopped a girl from getting raped... it didn't really occur to me that I had much to fear from you. You seem like you're from the right side, I just want to know why. Though it seems you're not the talkative type."

"I usually let other people do the talking. I'm more the action type," Recker said.

"So I've noticed. So, Michael Recker, why are you following me? Did my father put you up to it?"

"What's that?"

"My father. I figured it must've been him. The last time I talked to him a couple of weeks ago and told him about Stephen, he indicated I should do something about it."

"You did. You got a restraining order."

Hendricks rolled her eyes. "That thing? Hardly worth anything."

"Why do you say that?" Recker wondered.

"I work in a hospital. You know how many women I've seen walk, or wheeled in, that had restraining orders?"

"Then why'd you get it?"

"I don't know. Everyone kept telling me what a good idea it was, friends, family, people I work with... I guess I figured it was better than doing nothing, even if I didn't really think it was worth it," she said.

Recker nodded, understanding her reservations. "You

know, he's already violated that order, you could just call the police if he goes near you again."

"Why? So they can put him in jail for a couple of months. Then I have to worry about it all over again. It's like, why bother? It just keeps prolonging everything and it's never settled."

"I understand."

"So is it my father that hired you?"

"Uh, I'm not at liberty to reveal that kind of information. Why don't you ask your father about it?"

Hendricks groaned. "Yeah, like that would be any better. He would just deny it too."

"You two don't get along, I take it?" he asked.

"We get along fine as long as we don't see each other more than once a month," Hendricks said, smiling. "He's a big business executive. He's always been more concerned with his stock portfolio, or his vacation house, or the three BMW's he owns, than his own daughter. Money cures all problems according to him."

"I know the type. Don't confide in your mother much either, I take it?"

"She died when I was ten."

"Oh. I'm sorry."

"Yeah. She had cancer."

"And you and your father haven't been close since."

"Not really. I mean, I guess I understand, you know... what's a man who's not there most of the time know about raising a daughter on his own?"

"Sounds like he struggled."

"If he ever tried. All he did was hire babysitters and

nannies to watch me all the time, most of whom he probably slept with," she said, reminiscing.

"Sounds rough."

Hendricks shrugged. "Wasn't so bad I guess. I guess I turned out all right."

"So it seems."

"So what are you gonna do, just follow me around all day?"

"Not while you're at work," Recker sipped his drink.

"How long do you plan on doing this for?" she said.

"Until I'm sure your ex is no longer a threat to you."

"I'm sure he'll go away in a few days."

"Considering the threats he's made, I kind of doubt that's the case," Recker said.

"How do you know he's made threats? I didn't tell my father that. I just said I was having trouble with him."

Recker smiled. "I have my sources."

"Did you hack into my phone or something? Can you do that?"

Recker put his finger in the air, trying to deflect the question. "Uh, did you order yet?"

"Oh, no, not yet."

The waitress came over and took her order as the two continued discussing her situation.

"It doesn't seem like you're afraid of him," Recker stated.

Hendricks shrugged. "I'm not, really. I mean, he makes idle threats and all, but I don't really take them seriously. It's just him talking a big game like he always does."

"You know, a lot of women who end up dead or in the hospital... they probably said the same thing."

A more concerned look overtook the pretty nurse's face. "So you really think he means it then?"

"I think he's dangerous and I think you shouldn't overlook what he's capable of."

"Gee, I'm so glad I talked to you and put my mind so at ease," she said, faking a smile.

"I'm sorry, I didn't mean to scare you. But I just want you to understand how serious this is and not to underestimate him."

"So what if he doesn't do anything for a while, or just keeps up doing this for months? Are you just gonna keep following me?"

"I don't think it'll take that long. It's escalated for him. I'm pretty sure it's gonna come to a head soon enough."

"That doesn't sound appealing for me," Hendricks said.

Recker tried to give her a warm smile to reassure her. "Don't worry. That's what I'm here for. I'll protect you."

"Well, I'm sure you can't be near me twenty-four hours a day. What happens if he shows up when you're not around?"

Recker had a feeling about what she was intimating and thought it probably wasn't a bad idea. It certainly made his job easier if he didn't have to operate in the shadows. He took out a small notebook from his coat and tore out a piece of paper. He wrote his name and phone number down and slid it across the table to her.

"If you feel threatened, any time, day or night, you call me. Chances are I'll be nearby anyway," Recker said.

Hendricks looked at it and nodded, smiling at him. "Thank you." It wasn't the warm smile she gave earlier though. It was more along the lines of "I can't believe I have to go through all this."

Hendricks continued talking about her situation for a few more minutes. Even though Recker could hear what she was saying, he wasn't really listening intently. He was looking at her, thinking of how pretty she looked. She was pretty, not a bombshell, but she had that cute, girl next door vibe going on for her. She talked softly, had sexy eyes that could melt any man's heart who looked inside them, and had soft, jet black hair. She seemed to be pleasant and have a good personality, though not afraid to be bold if she had to be, evidenced by her approaching him to begin with.

Another time, another place, and Recker thought she was the kind of girl that would interest him. He could imagine getting lost in those eyes. He couldn't believe there was a man out there lurking around with the intention of hurting her. The more he talked to her, the more she spoke, the more he found himself liking her. After about an hour of conversing, Hendricks looked at her phone.

"Oh my gosh, I lost track of time," she said, making sure she had everything in her purse. "I'm gonna be late."

"Well this was fun," Recker said.

Hendricks grinned, picking up the playful sarcasm and

looked at him funny. "Really? Was I that bad company?" She gave as good as she got.

"Not at all," he said, shaking his head. "This will probably be the highlight of my day."

Hendricks stood up at the edge of the table. "Do I need to give you my itinerary?"

Recker smiled. "No thanks. I already have it."

She returned the smile. "I'm sure you do. Should I give you my plans for the day or the rest of the week?"

"I already have your work schedule."

"Why does that not surprise me? Well, after work, I'm going straight home, not stopping anywhere."

"Good to know."

"So will I see you again sometime? Or only if I look at the end of a parking lot and see you lurking in a car somewhere?" she said.

"Never know."

"Well, I guess I should say thank you for looking after me."

"There's no need."

She gave him that sweet smile of hers before leaving. "Well, hopefully we'll see each other again."

Recker smiled and raised a hand to say goodbye.

7

Recker and Jones had just had dinner in the office, fast food, as they'd often had in the past week. After finishing, they each went to different computers, working on different projects.

"Do you think it was wise to engage Ms. Hendricks in conversation?" Jones asked, typing on his keyboard.

"Well I didn't have much choice, David. She'd seen me on three different occasions and approached me. Not much I could do."

"And here I thought someone with your expertise and experience could avoid detection by a simple pediatric nurse,"

Recker didn't really have a comeback, "Hey, you made a joke." He gave Jones a look of mock annoyance. "I'm a little rusty OK! It's been a while."

"So it would seem."

Recker laughed. "Ouch!" He sat quietly tapping away at the keyboard before he spoke again. "It might work out for the better. It's always easier to keep someone under surveillance who knows what the stakes are and willingly knows and allows it."

"I just worry about your cover."

"It's fine. She thinks her father sent me to look after her. That should hold up since it doesn't appear that they're very close and don't talk often."

"I hope you're correct."

"Don't worry about her. She's fine."

"I'll take your word for it."

"Besides, she may come in handy for us after her case is over," Recker said.

Jones stopped typing and swiveled his chair around to look at his partner. "What do you mean?"

"She's a nurse, right?"

"I'm failing to see your point."

"At some point, a nurse might be a good idea to have around in case of emergencies."

"I don't know about that." Jones sounded worried.

"I dunno. I figure at some point, if we wind up doing this for years, it's a decent possibility that I might get hurt eventually, or even shot."

"And you think it'd be wise to bring Ms. Hendricks into the fold for that purpose?"

"Not bring her into the fold. She doesn't have to be in on what we're doing. Just keeping her as a contact in case of emergency. After all, me going to a hospital in such a case is risky business."

"You've gotten out of there before."

"How many times you think I can do that?"

"How did you do that in London, anyway?"

"Found a contact with a less than reputable reputation. I'll tell you about it another time. Let's just say he trusted the CIA even less than I did, which made him the perfect contact."

"Well, as far as Ms. Hendricks, I'll follow your lead. If you think she's necessary."

"Not necessary. Just someone we can trust. One thing you learn as a CIA black op is that if you don't have a few people you can trust when your life's in danger... you won't last very long."

Jones turned back to his computer and continued typing away, alternating between the laptop and the desktop. They kept banging away at their respective computers for several hours. Just as the time reached nine o'clock, Jones stopped, seeing something on the screen that stopped him in his tracks.

"Oh dear," Jones said suddenly, sounding deeply concerned.

"What's wrong?" Recker swung round on his chair to face him.

"It appears we have another situation on our hands and it looks gravely serious."

"What's up?"

"It would seem there's a woman whose life is in danger. A man too for that matter."

"What's going on?"

"Listen," Jones said, hitting the play button on his software program.

"I'm telling you right now, if I find her at that hotel

tonight with her boss, I'm gonna kill them." The strange voice sounded angry.

"That was the message that Martin Gilbert left on the voicemail of a friend of his," Jones said, filling in the first bit of detail.

"I take it the her he's referring to is his wife?" Recker said.

"That would be correct." Jones was feverishly typing away on the laptop. "His wife's name is Lorissa Gilbert."

Recker looked at the screen as Jones pulled up the DMV information of the husband and wife, picture included.

"Who's the boss?" Recker said.

"Hold on, getting that information now," Jones said, pulling up Lorissa's job info.

"Advertising agency secretary." Recker read the details off the screen. "Boss is Kevin Fitzpatrick. Where's that hotel Gilbert's talking about?"

"I'm trying to locate it now. But it sounds as if Mrs. Gilbert's having a late night rendezvous, perhaps not work related."

"You don't know that. Don't jump to the obvious conclusion," Recker said. "Maybe it is work related and this husband of hers is the super jealous type who also jumps to the wrong conclusion."

"Perhaps you're right. Maybe I am being too hasty with my judgment."

"How's that location coming?" Recker grabbed his coat, checked his weapons and was ready to go.

"Just about got it," Jones said, taking another minute to

find the spot while Recker hovered impatiently knowing that sometimes seconds can mean the difference between life and death. "There it is. Sheraton Hotel in Society Hill."

"What room number?"

"Three twenty-one. Registered to Kevin Fitzpatrick. And it looks like Mr. Fitzpatrick has already checked in."

"I'm on my way. Call me with whatever else you come up with," Recker shouted as he rushed out the door.

Recker drove the half hour it took to get to the hotel. As he pulled into the parking lot, Jones called him with more information.

"Mr. Recker, have you reached the hotel yet?"

"Just got here."

"I've come up with a few more details, one of which being that Martin Gilbert purchased a gun two weeks ago."

"What kind?"

"A Smith & Wesson forty caliber, it's…"

"That's all I need, I know it. Nice weapon."

"Yes, well, regardless of your fondness for it, I would imagine he's carrying it with him tonight."

"Gilbert have a record?" Recker asked.

"Not that I can find."

"I don't think I have to worry too much about him. Sounds like a novice."

"Just be careful with him. Anyone with a gun can be dangerous, especially if you take them lightly."

"Yeah, thanks for that." He cut the call. Like he needed telling.

Recker got out of his car and went inside the hotel,

immediately going to the elevator, stopping at the third floor. Without seeing anyone else in the halls, he walked down the hallway, stopping at three twenty-one. He stood there at the door, listening. He heard several voices. A man's voice was talking loudly, and somewhat incoherently, as well as a woman's voice, though it was mostly crying from her.

Recker tapped his earpiece. "Jones, he's already here. Sounds like something's about to go down. Looks like I'll have to step in."

Jones responded, his voice distorted in Recker's ear. "Do what you must."

Recker carefully turned the handle so as to not make any noise to alert the subjects in the room. He opened the door a hair, peeking inside to gauge where everybody was. The bed was in a small room to his right, and Gilbert's back was to him. He had a gun out and pointed at his wife, naked under the bed sheets next to her boss. They were holding each other, afraid for their lives. Recker slowly walked into the room, hoping the floor wouldn't creak underneath him and give him away. Amidst her crying, Lorissa looked over and saw Recker walking closer. Recker put his hand up to his face and moved it around, hoping she wouldn't give away his presence. Gilbert kept yelling at his nude prisoners, trying to get up the nerve to pull the trigger on the pistol he'd never fired before. He waved the gun around, taking turns on which person he pointed it at. Once Recker got within a few feet of him, he rushed him. Gilbert didn't realize he had company until Recker was right on top of him, the former CIA agent throwing him into the wall with a body block any NFL tight end would be proud of. Anytime you surprise someone who's holding a gun, and there's physical contact, there's a chance of the gun going off by accident. Luckily, Gilbert's finger wasn't on the trigger and the pistol flew out of his hand without incident. As Gilbert laid against the wall, stunned, and holding the back of his head which hit the bottom of the wall, Recker walked over to the gun and picked it up.

"Oh my God, thank you so much!" Mrs. Gilbert said, as her and her lover scrambled to put clothes on.

Recker looked away to one side. "If I were you two, I'd be more careful next time."

"We will."

"Or better... you... you might wanna see a divorce attorney. I might not be around next time," Recker said, smiling.

"Are you a cop or something?" Fitzpatrick asked.

"Not quite. You, call the police and tell them what just happened," Recker said, pointing at the boss.

Recker noticed Gilbert starting to move around and went over to him, punching him in the face, temporarily incapacitating him again.

"What are you doing?" Lorissa asked. She didn't seem upset that Recker was beating on her husband. Maybe the divorce attorney was a good idea.

"Making sure he doesn't wake up again," Recker replied.

He picked Gilbert up from behind, grabbing him underneath his arms, and dragged him along the floor across the room.

"Open up that closet," Recker told them.

Lorissa did as the stranger instructed and opened the closet door as her boss was on the phone with the police. Recker threw Gilbert into the closet and closed the door, locking it. He looked around and saw a chair, maneuvering it in front of the door to prevent it from opening, just in case Gilbert had a fit of rage and tried to plow through it.

"What are you doing now?" Lorissa asked again.

"Making sure he doesn't escape."

"Is that really necessary?"

"He was about to kill the both of you," Recker answered. "Do you really want to be here by yourselves when he wakes up?"

"Uh, no, good point. Aren't you staying with us until the police get here?"

"Sorry, don't have the time. I've got other things to attend to."

"Poor Martin," his wife said.

Recker rolled his eyes. "He was going to shoot you. Too late for pity now." Her reaction, belated as it was, made no sense to him and was beginning to aggravate him. "Listen. If he wakes up before the police get here, don't you even think about opening that door, no matter what he says."

"Don't worry about that, I'll make sure of that," Fitzpatrick replied, walking over to them. "Police should be here in a few minutes."

"Good. Next time you wanna screw one of your employees, you might wanna make sure their husband isn't the violent type," Recker said.

"Noted."

"Who are you?" Lorissa asked.

"Oh, just call me the silencer."

"What?"

"I'm just someone who silences problems."

Recker then left, eager to get out of the hotel before the police arrived. Once he got to his car, he stayed for a few minutes and watched to make sure none of the parties disappeared before the police got there. The cops arrived a little over five minutes later, Fitzpatrick and his lover still waiting in the room for the police. With the police being there, Recker's work was done. He drove out of the parking lot with the intention of going home. He figured he'd let Jones know he was finished as he drove.

"Jones, mission accomplished."

"Excellent, Mr. Recker. How did it go?"

"No problems. Gilbert's subdued, the wife and boss weren't harmed, police are there now. I'd say everything went off without a hitch."

"Excellent. What are your plans now?"

"I figured I might go home for the night. You know, get some sleep," Recker said.

"What about Ms. Hendricks?"

"She's still at work. She's going straight home after her shift is over."

"Do you think it'd be wise to cruise around her apartment just to make sure that Eldridge isn't waiting for her?"

"Why, is there something indicating he might be?" Recker said.

"Nothing specific. But his threats lately have been escalating. You already had a physical altercation with him and alienated him."

"And you're thinking it's gonna come to a head soon."

"That would be my guess. He thinks you might be her new boyfriend, or something along those lines. I would think you'll be seeing him again sooner rather than later."

"All right, I'll head over there for a bit. Once she comes home, I'll wait there for a couple of hours to make sure everything's safe and sound. After that I'll check out for the night."

Recker then proceeded to drive the forty-five minutes it took to reach Hendricks' apartment. It was a group of four-story buildings that housed a couple of hundred apartments. He drove into the lot where her building was and was startled to see her car parked there. She wasn't supposed to be home for another two hours or so. He got out of his Explorer and walked over to her car and felt the hood. It was still warm so she couldn't have been there long. She must've finished work early. Recker just casually turned his head, not looking at anything in particular, when more alarm bells started going off. Eldridge's pickup was there. Recker quickly ran over to it, hand on his gun, just in case Eldridge was in there and decided to make some trouble for him. Once Recker got to the truck, he looked inside. It was empty. Recker sighed and got Jones on the phone.

"Looks like my night's not over yet, Jones."

"What's the matter?"

"Mia's already here. Must've got done work early," Recker said.

"Why is that troubling?"

"Cause I also see Eldridge's truck... and he's not in it."

"Oh my. You better get up to her apartment," Jones told him.

Recker was already running. "I'm on my way."

Recker ran towards the apartment entrance and rushed down the hallway until he got to the stairs. It'd be quicker than waiting for the elevator. He quickly ran up the steps, skipping several at a time until he got to the fourth floor. He ran down the hall, stopping in front of Hendricks' door. From the commotion that was coming from inside the apartment, it appeared as if she was in trouble.

It sounded as if Eldridge was roughing her up.

She was pleading with him to stop.

Recker turned the handle to the door, but it was locked. He took a step back and kicked the door open with a loud crash as it opened and another as it smashed into the wall inside. One step inside Recker saw Hendricks laying on the floor with Eldridge standing over her, lunging down as if he'd just hit her.

When he saw the stranger who'd roughed him up once already, Eldridge jumped up and stepped back from his ex-girlfriend.

He had a gun in his waistband and reached around for it. He never got the chance to use it though, as Recker rushed into the room and speared him shoulder first in the gut, slamming him into the floor. The gun flew from Eldridge's hand as his body hit the ground.

The two of them wrestled on the ground for a minute,

exchanging a few punches. Once they got back to their feet, Eldridge attempted to land a couple of shots on Recker's face, though the former CIA agent blocked them. Recker returned the favor and had better luck, landing several punches to Eldridge's face, bruising him around his eye.

Hendricks had gotten back on her feet and went to the kitchen, standing by the counter to observe the action. She would've called the police if she had her phone but she didn't have a landline, and her cell phone was in her purse, which was on the other side of the room and there was no way she was going to interfere in the tussle between the two men.

After a few more minutes, Recker felt he was getting the upper hand and Eldridge was looking to escape. He fainted and dodged past Recker out through the smashed doorway and into the hallway. Recker took off in pursuit and followed him down the hall. He caught up to Eldridge as he reached the door to the staircase and the two of them scuffled as they burst through the door onto the stairs. Recker was the first to his feet and delivered another blow to the side of Eldridge's face, knocking him down the steps. Eldridge was dazed and struggled getting up. Recker slowly descended the steps, knowing he was now in full control of the situation.

He grabbed the back of Eldridge's shirt and helped the beaten man back to his feet, only to smack him around a few more times. Eldridge fell again, his back on the steps, and though he was woozy, came to the conclusion that the man in front of him had the intention of killing him. Since

Recker stood in front of him, blocking his access to the bottom of the stairs, Eldridge stumbled away from his attacker, going up to the roof in hopes of somehow getting away from him.

Recker kept following his victim up the stairs, though he didn't think it was necessary to hasten things, walking methodically up each step. Recker assumed his target had nowhere to go, unless there was some type of ladder on the side of the building to allow his escape, and knew Eldridge couldn't get away from him. Even if he did, Recker hoped the beating he had giving the man would be enough to teach him to steer clear.

As soon as Recker walked through the door to the roof, a big right hand from Eldridge caught him in the face sending him back a couple of steps. Though stunned for a split second, Recker shook his head and shrugged it off, going back on the offensive. He caught Eldridge with several more blows, the amount of punches now taking their toll on his body as he crawled along the floor. Once he got to the end, he pulled himself up by the concrete ledge that lined the rooftop.

Eldridge was able to turn himself around, breathing heavily from the punishment he'd absorbed, to face his attacker. He put his hands out, hoping to stop Recker from coming closer to him.

"Just wait," Eldridge pleaded, wiping blood off his forehead. "I have some money."

"Not interested," Recker replied, taking a step closer to his subject.

Eldridge coughed and looked around, hoping for

something he could use to fend off the man who seemed to be intent on killing him. There was nothing that would save the day for him. He looked over at the building next to them and knew his only chance would be to jump onto the roof next to them. It was a big gamble though. It was about eight feet away and he wouldn't be able to get a running start. With his injuries, he wasn't sure if his body was strong enough to make the jump. But he knew that without taking the chance, he was as good as dead anyway. He was positive that the man who'd beaten him so severely was going to kill him. His only chance at surviving was to jump to the adjacent roof and escape down the stairs.

Eldridge quickly mustered enough strength to get back to his feet, clambered up on the ledge and faced the neighboring building.

Recker stopped walking toward him, wondering what the man was planning. It looked as if he was thinking about jumping, but Recker didn't think he could make it. Recker stood and watched, deciding to let him take the risk if he was so inclined. Eldridge turned around to take one last look at Recker, who took a step forward. It was now or never. Eldridge took a step back, then hurled himself off the roof. He just barely reached the neighboring building, his fingers grazing the concrete ledge, unable to take hold of it. His nose was broken as his face smashed into the brick building and he fell the momentum of the jump turning him over mid-air. The back of his head and neck were the first parts of his body that hit the ground, and he died instantly, unable to survive the brutal impact of a forty-foot fall.

Recker looked on from the roof, staring down at the lifeless body of the man he'd just beaten to a pulp. He sighed and shook his head, unconcerned about Eldridge's death, but he knew it would complicate matters. Now, the police would come in and do an investigation. He wanted to grab a minute with Hendricks before the cops arrived to make sure she was OK. Recker rushed back down the stairs and down the hall, going into Hendricks' apartment. She was sitting on the couch, holding her head.

"You all right?" Recker asked, trying to close the door behind him the best he could.

Hendricks took her hand off her head, and looked up at him, relieved to see him. "Uh... yeah. Yeah, I think so."

"What happened?"

"I got done early from work. When I got here, I got to the door, and as I was unlocking it, he grabbed me. I didn't see him. I don't know where he was. I guess he was waiting for me." She looked down at her feet as she spoke.

"What then?"

"We started talking, and I told him to go and I didn't want to see him again. That made him mad. Really mad. He shoved me inside and started yelling at me and hitting me."

"That's when I walked in."

She nodded. "Yeah."

"Well, you won't have any more problems with him."

"You don't think he'll come back?"

"Not likely."

"How can you be sure?" she said.

MIKE RYAN

Recker sighed, knowing there was no good way of telling her. "He's dead."

"What?" Hendricks said, jumping up in disbelief.

"As we were fighting, he went up to the rooftop. I guess he figured his only chance of getting away was to jump to the next building. He didn't make it," Recker explained.

"Then you didn't kill him?"

Recker shook his head. "No. Can't say I didn't want to, but no. He did that on his own."

Hendricks looked disappointed, not that she wasn't happy to have Eldridge out of her life finally, but she didn't want anybody dead, even him. "So what now?"

"Police will probably be here soon."

"So what do we tell them?"

"You just tell them the truth and what happened. You'll be fine."

A peculiar look came over her face, as it sounded to her like he wasn't planning on sticking around. "You say that like you won't be here too."

Recker made an agonized face of his own. "I can't, really."

"Why not?"

He sighed, not wanting to get too involved. "It's complicated. The police can't know anything about me, even my name."

"Why?" Hendricks fixed him with a look. "I don't understand."

Recker knew he was in a difficult spot. He risked compromising himself whether he told her the truth or not. "Let's just say that the police may not believe that

130

someone like me didn't throw him off the roof instead of him jumping."

"Is that really what happened? Did you throw him off the roof?"

"No. What I told you is exactly what happened."

"Then I don't understand why you can't stay."

"I don't expect you to understand, but I can't."

"I'm scared," Hendricks said. Shock was starting to kick in now the adrenaline high was wearing off.

Recker put his arm around her to try to comfort her as best he could. "I know. Just tell them when they arrive that you don't know who the man was that helped you."

Still looking quite nervous, Hendricks still tried to get him to stay. "I just don't know what to do."

"You'll be OK. He can't hurt you anymore."

"Are you wanted by the police for something?"

"No. Not for the reasons that you'd think. I'm not a criminal or anything. There are bigger things at play that I don't have time to go into right now though," he said.

"What if I just tell the police that I fought him off and he left despondent? And that he went to the roof and jumped."

"Mia, you don't need to lie for me. You can just tell them what happened," he smiled. "Just conveniently forget my name."

Hendricks nodded, agreeing to his terms. Recker took his arm off her and started towards the door when Hendricks asked for a favor from him. "If I do as you ask, would you be able to meet with me tomorrow and explain what this is all about? Please?"

Recker sighed, knowing it was against his better judgment to agree to her request. But there was just something in her voice that he couldn't deny it. Plus, he was in a no-win situation. If she told the police his name it'd be just as bad as if he stayed and talked to them himself. "OK," he said.

"Can I call you in the morning?"

"Why don't I just meet you again for lunch at Joe's Diner at noon?" Recker said, "and don't mention that number to the police."

Hendricks nodded again. "OK. Thank you."

Recker left the apartment, making sure nobody saw him exit, and went down the stairs to the main floor. He walked out of the main entrance and noticed a crowd starting to gather around Eldridge's body. He went to his truck and just sat in it for a minute. His hands were scraped and bloody and when he looked in his rearview mirror he had marks and abrasions on his face. He didn't want to be there when the police showed up so he didn't waste any more time in staying there. He started driving to his apartment, calling Jones along the way.

"Jones, doesn't look like Eldridge is gonna be an issue anymore," Recker said.

"Why is that? Did he finally get the message?"

"Well, yeah, in a way. He's dead."

"Oh no. What happened?" Jones said. He sounded genuinely concerned.

"Fell off the roof."

Jones was temporarily stunned. "Fell off or was thrown off?"

"Fell off. Well... jumped to be precise."

"Excuse me for my apprehension, but didn't you say something about throwing him off a roof when we first started this case?"

"Oh, come on, I was only joking when I said that," Recker said. "Well, sort of."

Jones sighed, knowing this wouldn't help them to remain inconspicuous. "How is Ms. Hendricks?"

"She's fine. A few bumps and bruises from Eldridge before I got to him."

"Well, I'm glad she's not more seriously hurt. Why don't you go home and get some rest?"

"Thanks, I will. It's kind of been a long day."

"We'll discuss your methods further in the morning," Jones said sternly.

"Can't wait... Professor," Recker said.

8

Recker came into the office the following morning, breakfast in hand, hoping it'd help to smooth things over with Jones. He knew Jones probably wasn't happy with him in regards to Eldridge's death.

"Is this supposed to be a peace offering?" Jones said, taking his food.

Recker shrugged. "If you like."

"I can't be bought with food, you know."

"So what can you be bought with?" Recker couldn't resist trying to find out more.

"Nothing," Jones said, not taking his eyes off the computer screen. "Have you seen this?" he said, handing over a copy of the newspaper.

Recker sighed, sure he was about to find himself in there somehow. He immediately saw the headline of the situation that happened at the hotel involving the Gilberts.

"It appears the man in the trench coat has been nicknamed The Silencer," Jones stated. "Wonder how they came up with that."

Recker looked away from the paper and at his employer, chuckling to himself that the name stuck. "You know these media types. Just throwing names at the wall to see what sticks. Helps to sell papers. God knows where they get these kinds of ideas from," he said, rolling his eyes and pretending to know nothing about it. "Nothing about Mia in here?"

"Her situation was too late for the morning edition," Jones replied. "It is on the online version though since it's updated throughout the day."

"What's it say?"

"Here, you read it," Jones said, backing his chair away to let Recker read the article.

The article gave the account of what happened, with Eldridge forcing his way into Hendricks' apartment and roughing her up. It then stated that a man who was visiting someone else in the building walked by and intervened, leading Eldridge to become despondent and go up to the rooftop, where he then chose to end his life. The article gave a brief physical description of the stranger that interrupted the attack, though it didn't match Recker at all. It listed the stranger as being around 5'9, a hundred and eighty pounds, in his forties, slightly husky, a beard, and black hair that ran down past his shoulders. That was as far away from Recker's description as it could get. After he was finished reading, Recker stepped back from the computer, letting Jones get back in there.

"It would appear that Ms. Hendricks covered for you," Jones said.

A grin came over Recker's face. "Seems that way."

"Thank goodness for that. You've had a lot of publicity the last several days. We don't really need more of it."

"Better get used to it. Gonna be a lot more of it by the time we're through."

"Isn't there a better way to end these conflicts without being compromised?" Jones said.

"Sure there is."

Jones' face brightened. "Then why don't we do that?"

"Because that'd involve a sniper rifle and me killing the targets from a distance," Recker said through a mouthful of food. "Now, I don't personally have a problem with that, and actually would probably prefer it, but I assume that's not what you're going for."

Jones' face was a picture of disgust. He wiped imaginary crumbs off him as he spoke. "I was hoping to avoid killing... as well as making you a household name."

Recker shrugged and took another bite. "So, what's next on the agenda? Have another target?"

"I think I should have one by this afternoon," Jones replied, sliding his food away from him. He'd lost his appetite.

"Good. Need me for anything until then?"

"No, I don't think so. Why do you ask?"

"I told Mia I'd meet with her for lunch," Recker said.

"Mia. We're on a first name basis with Ms. Hendricks now, are we?"

"She wanted some answers about what happened last

night. Considering she covered for me and lied about me being there, I figured I owed that to her. Don't worry, I won't tell her about you or this place or our exact business."

"I'm not worried about that," Jones said, skeptical about Recker's newfound relationship.

"What then? I can tell it's something." He screwed up his wrapper and threw it at the trash bin. He missed.

"I wonder if perhaps you're getting too close to her. She does have a pretty face."

"I tried that once before," Recker said with a shake of his head. "I won't make that mistake again. Maybe she's a friend, maybe she's a contact, maybe she's someone we can use in case of emergency. But that's all she is and all she will ever be. Even if I wanted to, I'd never let another woman make the mistake of loving me. She deserves better than that. You not going to eat that?" Recker pointed at Jones' rapidly cooling breakfast and smiled.

Knowing it was still a touchy subject for him and noting the change of subject, Jones simply gave him a warm smile and nodded. He knew Recker was still hurting over what happened to Carrie and could tell it was a pain that wasn't likely to go away anytime soon. He just hoped it'd be a pain that didn't consume him. Since he had a few hours to kill before meeting Hendricks, Recker fiddled around on one of the computers, helping Jones to identify future victims for them to aid.

Once eleven o'clock rolled around, Recker excused himself and slipped out of the office for his lunch date. He got there about fifteen minutes ahead of schedule and waited in the same booth they met at the day before. While he was waiting, Recker ordered drinks for the both of them. Two cokes. That was his usual choice of drink during the day and he noticed that was what she had the last time they met. Mia came right on time, exactly at twelve, punctual as usual. As soon as she entered the diner, she immediately found her lunch date in the corner of the restaurant and sat down across from him. She flashed him that sweet, innocent smile of hers, though behind that smile was a boatload of questions that she wanted answers to.

She took a big breath before starting to talk. "I had fears, or visions, that I'd come and you wouldn't be here."

"Why would you think that?" Recker said.

"I don't know. Just had this thing where I thought you were gonna blow me off."

Recker shook his head. "I wouldn't do that. Not to you."

Hendricks smiled again. "I have so many questions," she said, not quite knowing where to begin.

"I know. Before we get to all that though, how are you?"

It looked like she was struggling to find an answer. "I'm uh... I'm OK, I guess."

"It's not an easy thing to have to go through."

"It's weird, you know? Umm, I'm glad, relieved that I'll never have to worry about being stalked, or followed, or hit, or anything like that."

"But..."

"But I feel... kind of sad. I once really cared for him and to know that he's no longer alive, it's just..."

"It's a lot to process." Recker finished off the thought.

"I guess so. I don't wish death on anybody, no matter what they've done. I just wish there'd been another way and things would've worked out differently," she said, feeling down.

"It's important to know that it's not your fault for what happened to him. He chose the path that led to his downfall. Nobody chose it for him and nobody else is to blame for the choices he made."

"I know. And I don't feel guilty or responsible or anything. I just wish things went a different way."

"That's because you're a good person. Only an idiot would want bad things to happen to people."

"Well, I don't know how good a person I am, but thank you anyway. By the way, what do you prefer to be called? Mike? Michael? Don't tell me you're one of those people that prefers to be called by their last name. That really irks me when people do that," Hendricks said.

"Mike or Michael's fine. Only my enemies call me Recker." He smiled.

"Good. I like Mike. Michael sounds too formal, not very personal."

"Whatever you prefer."

The waitress came over and took their order, both of them ordering burgers with fries. He ordered his without onions, drawing a comment from Hendricks.

"How do you eat a burger without onions?"

"Are you kidding? I don't know anyone who eats that stuff," Recker said, pulling a face.

"Uh, hello? I do!"

Recker smiled, amused at her sense of humor.

"So are you finally gonna tell me who you are?"

"You already know that."

"No. I know your name. But I don't know *who* you are," she said.

"What do you wanna know?"

"You can start by telling me who hired you to watch over me, and don't say my father because I called him this morning and he was quite convincing in telling me he had no idea who you were. I kind of believed him when he mentioned hiring a bodyguard for me after what happened last night. Now, I doubt he'd mention that if he had already hired someone, don't you think?"

Grinning, Recker thought of how he could explain the situation to her. "I work for a very secretive security firm."

"Why didn't you tell me that before?"

"You didn't ask."

"Yes I did."

"You assumed your father hired me and I just went along with it. I never confirmed it was true," Recker said.

"Kind of a dirty trick."

Recker didn't reply and just tossed his hands in the air, not disputing the charge.

"You know, I read something in the paper this morning about a man who thwarted an attempted murder at a hotel last night," Hendricks said, looking at Recker's attire. "He, uh, happened to be wearing a trench coat. I'm sensing a pattern."

"I think I told you this before... there's a lot of trench coats out there."

They concentrated on their food for a few moments.

"So, what can you tell me about this security firm of yours?"

"Nothing."

"Let's see... you saved me, a girl who was almost raped, someone else who was almost murdered, robberies, how do you get around so fast?"

"I get good intel."

"You have to tell me something. Anything."

"I work for a security firm who wants to help regular, everyday people with certain problems."

"If I use myself as a guide, I'd say you're not hired by those people. So how and why do you do it?" she asked.

"We have a sophisticated computer system that indicates when people might have certain problems then we act on it."

"But why? What do you get out of it? Money? You're disappearing from every scene so I know it can't be notoriety or fame."

"The owner of this security firm is very wealthy. We don't get anything out of it except for the satisfaction of helping people who need it," Recker said.

"So why are you hiding from the police?"

"I'm not really hiding from them, per se."

"Then what?"

Recker sighed, not really sure of another way to tell her without saying the truth. Hendricks could see that he was struggling to come up with an answer and was getting frustrated with the cloak and dagger act that he put up.

"Why won't you tell me anything?"

"Because anything I tell you could put you in danger."
Recker gave her the only reply he could.

"How?"

"It's complicated."

"Do I need to go to the police? Or start my own investigation?" Hendricks said.

"Why do you need to know?"

"Because I find you interesting. And I'd like to know something about the person who helped me. Is that so wrong?"

"No, it's not wrong."

"Then please just tell me the truth. Would it put me in more danger if I tried to find out on my own?" She was trying hard to wriggle it out of him.

"Probably. And me along with it."

"Then why don't you just tell me so I don't have to go through all that."

"You know, behind that pretty face and innocent smile of yours, you're a very stubborn woman," Recker said.

Hendricks laughed. "You're not the first person who's ever told me that before."

"Why does that not surprise me?"

"So are you going to tell me? Or do I have to find out on my own?"

Recker put his hand over his mouth and rubbed his face a couple of times as he decided how much to reveal.

"So why all the secrecy?" Hendricks said again, leaning forward in anticipation of the answer.

"If I were to tell you the truth, you probably wouldn't

believe it. If someone told it to me, I probably wouldn't believe it either."

"Let me be the judge of that."

"The real reason I don't want to have any type of police contact is because once I do, my name goes into the system. Once that happens, radars go off everywhere," Recker said.

"What's that mean exactly?"

Recker sighed, figuring it was easier to just tell the truth than continue to dance around the subject. Well, at least as much of the truth as he could divulge, which still wasn't much. But he figured if he'd give her a little snippet of information, that'd hopefully be enough to satisfy her curiosity. He looked up to the ceiling for a second before his eyes danced around to the rest of the restaurant. He knew there was a risk in telling Hendricks anything about what he once was, but he also knew that if she was being truthful in that she would try to find out on her own, it was safer for her if she found out from him. At least he could control what she knew. He'd just have to hope she was as trustworthy as he thought she was.

"I used to work for the United States government," Recker revealed.

"OK?"

"That's about all I can tell you," he said, not really expecting it to suffice.

"Seriously? You think that's going to be enough?" Hendricks responded.

"No, not really. Was kind of hoping though."

"Why are you so secretive? I'm not trying to give you the sixth degree. I just want the truth about who you are."

Recker took a deep breath as he continued remembering his past. "There are things that are happening that I just can't tell you. Not right now."

"You don't trust me. Do you?"

"It's got nothing to do with trust. If I didn't, I wouldn't even be here right now," Recker said.

"What is it then?"

"It's about keeping you safe."

"From what?" Mia's eyebrows raised.

"From people a lot more dangerous than Stephen Eldridge."

"Are you on the run or something?"

"It's a lot more complicated than a simple yes or no answer," Recker said.

"Try me."

Recker leaned forward and started talking more softly, looking around to make sure nobody was listening. "I was involved in a top secret government project."

"Was?"

"My involvement in that project didn't go exactly as planned. Someone decided that I was no longer necessary in that project and decided to terminate me."

"By terminate you mean..."

"I mean kill. Someone tried to kill me and now I'm here... trying to make a difference. While at the same time trying to stay out of the crosshairs," Recker said, leaning back.

"Wow."

"I'm not a criminal or a bad guy, but I know a lot of things that certain people would be worried about me revealing. Once my name goes into an official government system, alarm bells start going off, and it pops up on the CIA's radar."

"The CIA?" Hendricks asked.

Recker just nodded.

"So that means they would know where you are and would come after you again?"

"That's it." Recker nodded. "Crazy, huh?"

"Wow. I'll say."

"Now that I've told you I'm afraid I'll have to kill you," Recker said, stony faced.

"What?"

Recker let out a laugh, "Sorry, an old secret agent joke. Always wanted to say it one time."

"Oh," Hendricks said with a look of relief on her face.

"I've taken you into my confidence. For your protection and mine, you can't say a word about me to anyone. They've already killed people that were associated with me before. They won't hesitate to do it again. If they even knew we had this conversation right now, they'd kill you just for sitting here, regardless whether you knew anything or not."

"Nobody will ever learn about you from me." She looked a little worried now.

"Good. I'd hate to move to a new city already."

"Why would you move?"

"If you told anybody about me, I'd ditch my phone,

pick up a new name, new city, start all over again. That'd all be done by tomorrow morning." He grinned.

"You don't have to worry about me," Hendricks said.

"I know. I pretty much knew that when I read an article this morning about the mysterious man who helped fend off your attacker. Didn't seem to fit the description of me at all."

"Well, you said to keep you out of it. I figured the best way to do that was to say it was someone else."

"Police believe it?"

"Seemed to. I told them I didn't know who the man was. Must've been visiting someone else in the building."

They continued talking for another hour as they ate their lunch, Hendricks still ribbing him over his lack of an appetite for onions. She was fascinated by his life, or former life, and sought to hear more stories from his past, a past he wasn't as anxious to delve into. Luckily, he wouldn't have to duck the questions any longer. Still wearing his earpiece, Jones' voice came booming in.

"What's up, Professor?" Recker said.

"Back to that again, are we?"

"Don't forget, I have company right now." Recker fake smiled at Hendricks, who was listening to every word her companion was saying.

"Oh yes, I almost forgot. How is that going, by the way?"

"Just fine."

"Good. Well, we have a new situation developing and it is urgent," Jones sounded slightly flustered.

"What's up?"

"I've intercepted several text messages indicating a robbery is about to take place."

"How soon?"

"Two o'clock."

"Where?"

"Albert's. It's a small convenience store over on fifth. Can you get there in time?"

"Why not just call the police with an anonymous tip?" Recker asked.

"Because we act on the information we uncover. We don't pass it along and hope. What if they don't act or they don't get there in time?"

Recker nodded his head, agreeing. "OK. I'm on my way. How many people am I dealing with?"

"Three that I can definitely pinpoint."

"Armed?"

"I can't say for sure. Looking at their backgrounds, I would say that there is a distinct possibility," Jones said over the clatter of fingers on the keyboard.

"OK. On my way."

Recker was already done with his meal and asked for the check, which he promptly paid. "I'm afraid I have to go," he said.

"Off to save the day somewhere else?"

"Something like that."

"Will I see you again soon?" She hoped she would.

"I don't know. I'll call you."

"Well, wherever you're going... be careful."

Recker smiled and walked away. He sped out of the parking lot and drove as quickly as he could to get to

Albert's. He got there about ten minutes before two. It was a small family owned store. Recker walked in and was immediately greeted by an elderly man, probably in his early sixties. He was standing behind the register, no glass or bars separating him from the customers he checked out. He was slightly overweight, wore glasses, and was mostly bald except for a small patch of gray hair on the sides of his head.

"You Albert?" Recker asked.

"Just like the sign says." The man replied with a cheerful laugh.

Recker took a quick look through the aisles to see if anybody else was in the store, either regular customers, or the three crumbs that were about to knock the place over. After going through the six small aisles, Recker went back to the front of the store, where the register was located.

"You might wanna take a break," Recker told him.

"Excuse me?"

"You're about to be robbed."

"What? Are you drunk or high or something?" Albert asked.

"Nope. You keep a gun under there?" Recker asked, his eyes pointing to under the register.

"Maybe." The storekeeper was getting a little uneasy about the stranger's questions.

"Three young kids are coming here in a few minutes with the intention of robbing you," Recker informed.

"How you know this? You a cop?"

"Close enough. You got a place you can hide out till this is over?"

"Uh, there's a bathroom and an office in the back. What are you gonna do?" Albert came out around the counter.

"I'm gonna pretend to be you," Recker said, stepping behind the register.

He looked down under the counter and found Albert's gun, a Sig Sauer 9mm. Recker picked it up and handled it for a second, aiming it toward the wall. He smiled and handed it over to its rightful owner.

"Nice choice."

"What do you want me to do?"

"Go back to the office or bathroom and hide out there. Take the gun with you just in case."

"You want me to take them out from back there?" Albert asked.

Recker smiled, impressed with his willingness to get in the fight. "No, I'll take care of them. If shooting starts, just make sure you're not in the line of fire. But just in case one of them gets a lucky shot off, be prepared to defend yourself if the need arises."

"You mean if one of them shoots you then searches the store for other people?"

"You got it."

"OK. If that happens, where should I shoot them? I know how to use it but I never had to fire a gun before. Wing them in the arm or leg or something?"

"If you have to shoot, shoot to kill. Center mass," Recker said, pointing to the middle of his chest. "Or, if you're close enough, right here." He showed him, putting his index finger in the middle of his forehead. "A winged or injured man can still kill you. If you ever fire that thing, you shoot to finish the fight."

"Gotcha," Albert said, walking to the back of the store. Just before he got to the office he turned around. "Is the backup team coming soon?"

Recker smiled. "It's just me. You're the backup team."

Five more minutes went by. It was a minute after two o'clock. Not a single customer entered the store in the time Recker had been there. Then the door swung open. Three young kids, probably in their late teens or early twenties, walked through the door. They all had sports caps on and baggy clothes, with a gun most likely nestled in the waistbands of their pants. Recker closely eyed them up as they all came in. As soon as the first one saw Recker, he stopped and did a double take, then nudged the second man in the arm to alert him. They weren't counting on anybody else other than Albert being there. They'd been in the store a few times before and never saw anyone else working there. Recker was a new wrinkle in their plans.

"Yo man, who you?" One of the kids spoke up first.

"Just an employee," Recker said.

"Where's Albert?"

"Oh, he took a lunch break."

The three men separated and walked throughout the store, making sure they were all alone. Recker could tell they were the three that Jones was talking about. A common technique of criminals that worked in pairs or teams was that they would spread out, especially in smaller stores or places without a lot of eyeballs on them, knowing you couldn't watch all of them at once.

One of the kids walked up to the register and started talking to Recker, while the other two moved around the counter.

"I'm sorry, you two aren't allowed back here," Recker said, facing the pair.

While he was talking to the others, the one in front of the register pulled a gun, pointing it squarely at Recker's body. Recker faked being surprised and began putting his hands in the air.

"Get the cash," The one with the gun gave out the instructions. Must be the brains of the outfit.

They started to move but quickly stopped when Recker brought his left hand down and kept it in the air in front of the two, directing them to stop.

"You guys don't really wanna do this, do you?" Recker knew what the answer would be.

"Yo dude, shut up and move out of the way and you won't get hurt," the gun toting man said.

Recker gave a half smile, "Well, I just wanted to give you a fair warning."

"Fair warning for what?"

Recker quickly reached into his opened coat and grabbed a pistol with each hand. He brought his hands out of the insides of his trench coat, pointing a pistol in both directions that the robbers were standing in. "Like I said, you really don't wanna do this?"

"Hey man, we ain't armed." One of the two to Recker's left spoke up.

"So why don't you guys just pack up and move on out of here before someone gets hurt?"

"We will. As soon as we get what we came for." The one with the gun was back in charge.

"Well, I don't think that's happening."

"There's three of us, man. There's only one of you."

"You got one gun, I got two," Recker said calmly.

As soon as Recker took his eyes off the two to the left, one of them reached into his jacket and pulled out a pistol. Recker looked back at him as he was removing it, shooting him in the chest. He turned back to the man in front of the register and blew a hole through him before he got a chance to do the same to him. Both men were dead as soon as they hit the ground. The third man in the crew really wasn't armed and hadn't made a single motion in any direction as he froze himself the moment the action started, not wanting to make a wrong move.

"I really ain't armed," the remaining robber said, putting his arms up, worried that he was soon going to join his friends.

"Lift your jacket up and turn around," Recker told him.

The kid did as was requested, revealing that he really didn't have a weapon on him. As he was spinning around, Albert came out of the office after he heard the shots. He saw Recker with a gun pointed at the remaining member of the crew.

"He one of them?" Albert said.

"Yeah. Call the police and tell them you're holding a suspect."

"You got it," Albert said, going over to the phone.

"Looks like you picked the wrong set of friends, kid," Recker said.

"They ain't my friends, really. They said they had this thing going on and it'd be easy money," he told him, shrugging.

"There's no such thing as easy money. There's your first lesson right there."

"Cops are on the way," Albert said, coming back over. "Should be here in just a couple of minutes."

"That's my cue to leave," Recker said.

"What? You have to tell the police what happened."

"Nah. You can do that for me. The two dead ones drew guns. You tell them I defended myself and shot them in self-defense. Make sure you tell them this one here wasn't armed. That's about all I can do for you, kid."

The kid shrugged, knowing he was screwed no matter what.

"Well, I gotta go," Recker said.

"Hey," Albert said, putting his hand out. "Thanks for everything."

Recker returned the handshake. "You take care."

"Don't be a stranger. You come back sometime, hear?"

Recker nodded and smiled. "I'll do that."

Recker quickly exited the store and walked down the street, staying close enough to see the store's entrance, just to make sure the third robber didn't get the jump on the elderly storekeeper before the police arrived. Three police cars came storming in only a minute later to take control of the situation. As Recker continued walking to his truck, he let Jones know the problem had been eliminated.

"Professor, situation's resolved," Recker said.

"Is there someone else with you?"

"No."

"Oh. Your use of the nickname threw me off," Jones said.

"What's the matter? Don't you like it?"

"I hadn't really given it much thought until now. Anyhow, what happened at the store?"

"Robbery thwarted, one in custody, two men down," Recker said, hurrying away at the sound of sirens.

"And Albert?"

"Safe and sound."

"Now, when you say two men down, you mean...?"

"I mean dead."

"I had an inkling that was your meaning. There was no other way to prevent it I assume?"

"If there was another way, I would've done it another way. You send me into a robbery that's about to happen with guys who have guns, what did you expect the result would be? Talk them into giving themselves up?"

"Yes, I know. It's just I wanted us to stop bad and violent things from happening and it seems as though we're just contributing," Jones said, sounding like he was having second thoughts about the whole operation.

"There's a difference. We're stopping bad things from happening to good people. The violent things are happening to the people who want it that way," Recker said.

"I suppose you're right."

"When we started, you told me sometimes you'd disagree with the way I handled things but knew I'd probably be right. These are some of those times. Trust me when I say there was no other way to handle these issues."

"I know. It doesn't always seem like the clean victory I was hoping for when I started this endeavor," the professor said.

"One thing I've learned over the years, is there is no clean victory. For anybody. Even the winners and the good people with the best of intentions wind up with blood on their hands. It's a product of the system. Be proud of what we've accomplished in a short time so far. We saved Mia from an abusive and violent ex-boyfriend; Gilbert and her boss from possible death at the hands of her husband; a store robbery that could've ended in Albert's murder if it went down differently; and a woman from being raped. Sure, a couple of people died in the process, but they weren't the people we were trying to save. They're the people who can't be saved and what we're protecting people from."

"When you put it like that it does lift my spirit's a bit. We have made a difference so far, haven't we?"

"We have. You're a big part of that. I'm the one on the street level but nothing I do is possible without you and your intel. You should feel proud of that."

9

A week had passed since the robbery attempt at Albert's went down. In that time, Recker and Jones had saved two more people from being killed, another robbery attempt, as well as an attempted arson. Recker had just arrived at the meeting spot he engineered with his contact along the Schuylkill River. He walked along the trail until he saw the statue, then waited along the metal railing by the river. He checked the time on his phone. He was about ten minutes early. Though it was a little cold, it was basically a pleasant day since the sun was out, so he didn't mind the wait so much. Fifteen minutes went by until his visitor finally arrived. Recker was leaning on the railing and looking at the river when the man put his hands on the railing next to him.

"You're looking healthy," the man said by way of a greeting.

"You look the same as when I saved you from that mob hit man in Sicily."

The man smiled, nodding. "Philadelphia, huh? Living here these days?"

"No. Told you. Cleveland."

"Oh yeah, that's right. Cleveland," the fifty-year-old former CIA agent replied, not believing it. "Just picked a neutral spot, right?"

Recker turned his head and smiled, realizing his former mentor knew him too well. "How's Boston?"

"Ahh, you know, takes a little while to get used to. The accents there drive me crazy, but what are you gonna do, you know? So what's this all about?"

"The less you know the better off you are. You're out of the game. I don't want you to get pulled back in," Recker said.

"What do you think you're doing by having me here?"

"You could've said no."

"I always had a weakness when it came to you," the man said. "I always gave you a long leash."

"Why was that?"

"Because you were a great student. And a good friend. And probably because you always reminded me of myself when I was a little younger."

They stood there for another minute, neither of them saying a word, just staring out at the water.

"They're still looking for you, you know," the former agent said.

"Figured they would be. You don't just try to terminate someone then forget about them after you've failed."

"They talked to me after London."

"When?" Recker said.

"Couple of days later. Wanted to know where I thought you might've gone. Told them I had no idea."

Recker smiled. "You always had that ability to make people believe anything you told them."

"Wasn't hard with them. I knew they were telling me some bullshit. Said you went rogue and were doing your own assignments off the grid. I've known some agents over the years who I thought could've gone over the edge but you weren't one of them. Especially not since you had Carrie. You'd never have done that to her."

A painful look of agony overtook Recker's face as he looked down, thinking of her. "Yeah. You took a big chance helping me out like you did. I can probably never repay you for it."

"You don't have to. You've already repaid me plenty over the years."

"How you figure that?" Recker looked over at the older man.

"By being my friend. It's just a good thing you contacted me after you left that hospital in London."

"Well, I had nobody else I could contact. Nobody I trusted anyway. You were the only one I knew who wouldn't betray me."

"Never," the man said, putting his hand on Recker's shoulder. "I'm just glad I still had that guy there who took you in. He owed me a favor. Saved his mother from a rather gruesome end."

"Yeah, he told me. Sorry about blowing your hold on him over me."

"That's all right. He still owes me another one." The man laughed. "Saved his girlfriend too."

Recker looked over his shoulder, uneasy about someone else being around. "Sure you weren't followed?"

The man took a step back, faking being insulted. "Who you think you're talking to here? I know they still might be watching me in case you contact me. Took a train to New York, then hopped a different one here. We're fine."

The former agent took a large manila envelope out of his pocket and handed it over to Recker. Recker quickly opened it and took a peek inside, seeing a picture of Jones.

"That the guy you're looking for?"

"That's him." Recker nodded.

"What makes you think he can help you?"

"I hear he's good with computers."

"Yeah, if you can find him. Even the NSA doesn't know where he is. You know he's good when he disappears even from them."

"That's why I want him. I hear he can bypass just about anything," Recker said.

"Assuming you can find him. And assuming he's willing to help you."

"I can be convincing."

"What makes you think you can even find him?"

"I have a couple of leads to check out."

"Like what?"

"You know I can't tell you."

"You know you don't need him," his friend said. "Give me a couple of weeks. I'll find the name of that son of a bitch that killed..."

Recker shook his head. "I know you would. But I don't want to put you in danger. You've already done enough. If you go poking around and asking questions then they're gonna know what you're doing. There's no other reason you'd be doing it other than helping me. They'd kill you for sure."

"Let me take that chance."

"No, I can't let you do that. Not with having Jenny and the kids. You have a life with them to look forward to. You gotta put them first. Definitely before me," Recker said. "Don't worry about me. I'll find what I'm looking for."

"I know you will. If you ever need anything else, don't hesitate to call me."

"I will."

The two former agents shook hands and went their separate ways. Recker walked back to his truck and sat in it as he opened the envelope and started reading its contents. It was a report about Jones, including a small picture of him, as well as his background information. It listed his real name and everything he did for the NSA, as well as his personal information from his time before being employed by the agency. The report had him as being missing and a red alert was listed for him, the NSA still looking for his whereabouts. Everything Jones had told Recker was down there in the report. He'd been truthful about everything. No discrepancies that Recker noticed. He continued reading the report for half an hour, rereading it several times until he was sure he'd looked over every inch of it to make sure he didn't miss anything. Once Recker was satisfied that he'd looked over the report long enough, he put the information back in the envelope. After reading Jones' information, and seeing that it was as he said it was, Recker felt a little better about his situation. That small nagging feeling in Recker's gut that said maybe Jones was another in the line of people who would betray him started to fade away.

Seeing as how Jones didn't have any other assignments for him at the moment, Recker drove back to his apartment to relax for a little while. He had an average-sized place, nothing too big since he was usually on a job and not here that often. Since Recker tried to avoid most people, he chose an apartment that had its own entrance. He had the upstairs apartment in a two story building. It was a one bedroom place that he had minimally furnished, just a bed, a TV, a couple of couches and a few tables. He had a corner desk in the living room with a couple of laptops on it in case he needed to work away from the office. It was comfortable enough for him, though for the average person, it probably would've seemed a little cold and impersonal. There wasn't even a single picture on the wall.

Recker didn't get too many days off since Jones could give him an assignment at a moment's notice, but he never really minded, at least not yet. Since he had nothing else of much interest in his life, work was really all he had. At least until baseball season arrived. The nation's pastime was one of the few things in life that he really enjoyed. It didn't matter what team, there was nothing quite like watching a baseball game. It was one of the only things that really relaxed him and got his mind off his troubles. Since he traveled so much over the years, he didn't really have a favorite team; he was mostly just a fan of the game. But since he was now in Philadelphia, and it seemed as though he might be there a while, maybe he'd throw in with the hometown team. He sat at his desk for a couple of hours, searching through the MLB website, reading stories, and getting ready for the upcoming season.

About halfway through the afternoon, though, his day off was cut short. Jones had called him and asked him to come to the office as quickly as possible. He sounded like it was an emergency. Recker figured it was another murder in the making that he'd have to stop. Since he had no external ties to slow him down, he was out of the apartment in just a couple of minutes. After making the half hour trek to the office, once he entered, he could see by the expression on Jones' face the seriousness of the matter.

"From your voice it sounded pretty urgent," Recker said. "Who's getting knocked off and when?"

"The urgency is immediate as you have correctly surmised. It is not a murder, however."

"Then what is it?"

"A kidnapping," Jones' face betrayed his fear.

"Who is it?"

Jones stopped his typing and looked at Recker stony faced. "It's a child. A little girl."

"What do you have?"

"A little girl named Mara Ridley was taken sometime this morning."

"Where?"

"Happened at their home on Spruce Street," Jones said.

"What happened?"

"As far as I can tell, Mara's parents went to work, left Mara in the care of their nanny, as is per their usual, then around ten o'clock someone knocked on the door and forced their way in and took Mara."

"The police in on it?"

"No, they've been instructed to keep the police out or they'll kill Mara immediately and won't even bother asking for money. They are complying with that request."

"How'd you pick up on this?" Recker looked over Jones' shoulder at the information on screen.

"A few minutes after it happened, they called Mr. Ridley on his cell phone. He is a financial analyst and apparently couldn't get to his phone so the kidnapper left a message. That's how the system picked up on it. Take a listen," Jones said, playing the voicemail.

"Mr. Ridley, as of ten minutes ago, we're now in possession of your lovely daughter. Call your home to verify what I say. Our terms for you getting her back are that we want one million dollars in cash three days from now. If you call the police, the FBI, or involve anyone else in this, trust us that we'll know. If you call the authorities, we won't call again, we won't negotiate, and you won't see your daughter alive again. We'll just send her home in a box... in pieces. If you value her life, don't play games with us," the kidnapper said.

"He's using plural, so it's not a one-man operation," Recker said. "What do his parents do?"

"Father's a financial analyst. Mother's an executive for a large drug company."

"They have the ability to pay?"

"Yes. They have a million dollar home, a large bank account, and sizable assets in a brokerage account."

"Well if they don't have a million in their bank account, it's gonna take time to sell off their assets," Recker said. "They haven't contacted police?"

"No. I've tapped into their phone logs and engineered my way into their computer with a virus, one that won't harm them, and they've done as requested and not contacted anyone."

"Only child?"

"Yes. As soon as Mr. Ridley heard the message he called home, though call logs indicate he didn't speak to anyone. He then called his wife and the two of them raced home." Jones was staying calm.

"Nanny was most likely tied up until they got there. How old is the girl?"

"Four."

"Any security cameras on site?"

"If only it were that simple. They do but the house completely lost all power five minutes before the kidnapping."

"If they're true to their word that they'll know if the Ridley's contact anyone, then that must mean they either have the house under surveillance or they have their phones tapped or both."

"You don't think they're bluffing?"

"Maybe. But when a child's life is at stake... you don't take chances."

"Through the spyware I installed on their computer, it appears that Mr. Ridley has already sold some of his assets."

"Stocks?"

"Yes. Sell order's already gone through. It'll take a few days to settle into his account though," Jones said.

As Jones feverishly continued typing away, trying to find out all he could about the family, Recker leaned back in his chair and put his hand on his forehead, thinking of the possible scenarios.

"Can you pull up pictures of the area?" Recker said.

"Thanks to our friend, Google, yes we can. What are you looking for in particular?"

"Anything in the area where someone could see the house if possible."

"You mean a lookout?"

"Yeah."

Jones did a three-sixty with the pictures of the area, but it didn't appear to do much good. Recker sighed, not satisfied with their findings. "I was hoping for an empty building, an office, or an apartment or something," Recker said, sounding frustrated. "Just other homes across the street."

"Well, on the outside at least. Let me verify that none of those are vacant."

"I'm gonna go there and take a look around and talk to them."

"Are you sure that's wise?" Jones asked, concerned about his presence there.

"I'll just walk around the area first and gauge the situation."

"I'll keep digging and let you know if I find anything of value. I'll have to figure out a way to talk to them somehow."

"How about by phone?"

"I thought you just said their phones might be tapped?"

"The far side drawer there." Jones pointed.

Recker went to the last drawer at the end of the desk and opened it, revealing five phones. "What's this?"

"Prepaid cell phones," Jones said. "I figured we should stock up on some in case of emergencies. If you could somehow get one of them to one of the Ridley's, that would solve the issue of potential phone tapping."

"You know, you're sneakier than you appear," Recker joked.

Jones went into another drawer and took out a small square device and held it in his hand. "Here, you might need this."

"What is it?" Recker asked, taking it from his hand.

"It's a listening device. If you touch base with Ridley, convince him to put this on his phone, and if the kidnappers call, we can hear their conversation."

Recker put the device in his pocket, then grabbed one of the phones from the drawer. He then left the office in order to go to the Ridley residence. He drove half an hour to get there and found an empty parking spot along the street on the same block as the Ridley house. He got out of his truck and milled around on the sidewalk, not getting too close to the house yet. At first, he just wanted to get a sense of the surroundings and see if he could notice anyone else that might've been eyeballing the house besides him.

He walked down the street, past the Ridley house, glancing in cars as he passed them by to see if anyone was in them. Once he walked a couple of blocks, he came back up the street, taking notice of nearby buildings and windows, not to mention the rooftops. He didn't notice anything suspicious, but he couldn't be positive. He didn't want to just go up to the Ridley house and have alarm bells start sounding if someone was watching.

He figured he'd do the next best thing to avoid suspicion. He went door to door, pretending to put something in the mailbox, hoping to pass for a salesman or marketer of some kind. He didn't knock on any doors or talk to anybody. This way, if someone was watching him, if he went to every house, they wouldn't suspect him of helping the Ridley's. Once he got to the house, he knocked very loudly and hit the buzzer on the door. He then put the phone down on the ground in front of the door and walked away. Recker walked a couple of blocks until he came to a coffee house and went inside, where he called the phone that he just dropped off.

"Hello?" the man's voice hesitantly answered.

"Mr. Ridley?"

"Yes. Who's this?"

"A friend."

"Are you one of the ones who has Mara?"

"No. I'm here to help you get her back. Meet me down

the street at the coffeehouse. I don't want to be seen around your house in case they have someone watching," Recker told him.

"How do I know you're not setting me up for something?"

"The only thing I want is to help get your daughter back."

"They said no cops," Ridley said.

"I'm not a cop."

"Then who are you? How would you know about this if you're not working with them?"

"Come meet me and I'll explain it to you."

"Why do I need to? As soon as I give them the money, they'll give me Mara back anyway," Ridley said.

"That's a very big leap of faith you're taking. Putting a lot of trust in the words of criminals who just abducted your daughter."

"What other choice do I have?"

"Let me help. Maybe I can find them and get Mara back before you give them the money," Recker said.

"What if it goes wrong and they do something to her? I can't take that chance. If it was my life, maybe, but not with hers."

"What happens if you give them the money, then after they have it, they kill the both of you?"

"Why would they do that?"

"Because you didn't involve police or anybody on the outside," Recker said. "They could kill anyone with knowledge of the kidnapping after they get the money and the police would never know there was one."

Ridley was silent for a few seconds, thinking about the situation. He didn't know what to do. All he wanted was for Mara's safe return. He initially thought as long as he paid the money, they would give her back. But if the stranger he was talking to was to be believed, after the kidnappers got the money, they might kill her anyway.

"Where are you again?" Ridley said finally agreeing to a meeting

"Coffee house down the street."

"When?"

"Now."

"How will I know you?"

"I'll know you," Recker said. "As soon as you walk in, turn to your left. I'm the third table."

"I'll be there in a few minutes."

Ridley wasted no time in getting there. He didn't even tell his wife what he was doing. He just told her he was going to get a coffee, not wanting to either upset her or get her hopes up. He walked the couple of blocks to the coffee shop, taking about ten minutes to get there. Ridley walked in and immediately looked to his left, seeing a man in a black trench coat sitting by himself and drinking a coffee, three tables down. Ridley cautiously approached the table, not quite sure what he was getting into, and nervous that the man wasn't really there to help him. Recker saw him as soon as he walked in the building and took a sip of his coffee as Ridley reached the table. Ridley moved a chair out and sat down, waiting for the other man to say something. Recker could see the fear in his eyes as he sat across from him. Not of him, though. Fear of losing his daughter.

"If you're not working with them, how do you know what's happening?" Ridley said, breaking the silence.

"I have resources that alert me to difficult problems where the police are not concerned."

"I don't really understand what that means."

"I know, but I don't really have time to explain it to you. The longer we sit here the longer it takes me to find your daughter," Recker said.

"Why do you want to help? What's it gonna cost me?"

"Nothing. I don't want anything from you."

"Then why would you be doing this?"

"I'm already employed by a public security firm. I go to work when things get tough,"

"What if they followed me here?"

"They would probably think you're getting coffee. There's no cops, we're not next to a window, you're fine. Besides, I canvassed the neighborhood and didn't see anything out of the ordinary."

"So they're not watching?" Ridley shook his head.

"Well, I can't guarantee that they're not so we'll just go under the assumption that they are just to be safe."

"So what are you gonna do?"

"First, do you have any idea who might be behind this?"

"No," Ridley answered with another head shake. "No one."

"Friends? Relatives? Co-workers? Anybody who's threatened you before? Anything?"

Continuing to shake his head, Ridley couldn't think of anyone. "My wife and I have banged our heads against the wall all day trying to think of something. Neither of us can come up with anyone."

"There has to be a connection somewhere. Neither of you are famous so it's not like they saw you on TV or something. Somewhere along the way, someone became aware of your situation and thought it'd benefit them."

"But who?"

"Anyone come to the house in the last couple of months to do work on it? Cable guy, electrician, anybody?" Recker asked.

Ridley leaned on the table with his hand over his mouth, racking his brain to remember. "Not that I recall."

"Difficult clients? Anybody unhappy with your work and maybe threaten you or anything?"

"No. Nothing."

"Recognize the guy's voice on the phone? The one that left the message."

"No," Ridley said, shaking his head.

"Involved in anything political? Maybe your views on something pissed someone off?"

"No. My wife and I work, then we come home to our family. No outside clubs or anything like that."

"Personal grudges, affairs, angry relatives that have been locked up or anything?"

Ridley shook his head again, "still nothing. Like I said, we've been over this all day, we can't come up with anything."

"What about the nanny?"

"Meghan? What about her?"

"What do you know about her? How long has she been working for you?"

"You don't think she's mixed up in this, do you?" Ridley looked shocked at the thought.

"I don't know. I'm just trying to find a connection or a link somewhere. If it's not with you, maybe it's with her."

"She's a sweet girl. I can't imagine she'd be mixed up in something like this."

"Maybe she is and doesn't know it," Recker said patiently. "Maybe it's someone from her past or background who knew her and found out who she was working for and thought it'd be an easy score."

"I hadn't thought about that. I just assumed it was because of us."

"Well, it might be. We have to consider all the possibilities though. How do her and Mara get along?"

"Great," Ridley shrugged. "She's great with Mara, and Mara loves her."

"Does she take Mara out sometimes for any reason?"

"Yeah, occasionally, you know, the park, toy store, bookstore, just walk around the block, things like that."

"How'd you hire her?"

"She was recommended by friends of ours. She watched their child for a few months last year and they told us she was great with kids."

"So she hasn't been with you that long?" Recker asked.

"Uh, no, about eight or nine months I'd say."

"Who watched Mara before her?"

"Well, my mother watched Mara during the day for the first couple of years, then she got sick and passed away.

Then we hired a woman who worked for us for about six or eight months," Ridley said.

"What happened with her?"

"Well, we thought she might've been stealing things. Nothing big, just small things. We thought she might've been taking things and selling them. And we got the feeling she wasn't being honest. You know, if I gave her twenty dollars to take Mara out, I thought she might've been spending like five of it and pocketing the rest."

"So you fired her?"

"Well, it was nothing heated or anything like that. We just told her we didn't think it was working out and wanted to go in a different direction. Plus Mara didn't really like her that much."

"What's her name?"

"Deanna Ambersome."

"Have her address or phone number?" Recker had his phone out ready to take on the details.

"Uh, not on me, no. I can get it though. I think we have it back at the house."

"OK. I want you to go back home and get her information for me. When you get it, you call me on the phone I gave you with the number that's in there."

"You don't want me to just go get it and come back?"

"No. Coming back here again would be suspicious if someone's watching. Just use the phone I gave you. It's not traceable and they don't know you have it. If you think of anything else, no matter how small or trivial, I want you to contact me."

"OK," Ridley said. "What are you gonna do now?"

"Now I'm gonna do some background investigation."

"On Meghan and Deanna?"

"It's a start."

"Will you let me know if you find anything?"

"You'll hear from me. Just keep doing what you were doing like I wasn't involved."

"Should I let my wife know?"

"That's up to you. There's one more thing," Recker said, digging into his pocket, taking out the listening device and showing it to Ridley.

"What's that?"

"It's a listening device. Put it on your phone when you get home. When the kidnappers call again, we'll be able to hear what they say. We also might be able to get a line on where they're calling from."

"I just can't believe this is happening. You hear about things like this... but you never dream it'll be you," Ridley said, taking the square device out of Recker's hand.

"I'll get her back for you. You weren't picked at random. Someone knows something or is involved somehow. I'm gonna find out who."

10

Recker and Jones spent most of the night finding information on both Meghan Carkner and Deanna Ambersome. They worked up until midnight before calling it a night. The following morning, Recker got back to the office about five. He figured he would've beat Jones in. He was surprised that when he got there, Jones was already knee deep in work.

"And here I thought I was gonna beat you in for once," Recker said.

"Perhaps if I had actually left, you would've accomplished your goal."

"You mean you've been here working all night?"

"Well, I went on the couch for two or three hours." Jones' baggy eyes told the story just as well as words.

"I thought when we left last night that you were leaving right after me?"

"That was my intention. But I just couldn't tear myself away. There's a little girl's life that may be at stake. Me losing a few hours of sleep is hardly significant compared to that. I can always catch up after this case is over. Besides, that was one of the reasons I got the couches in here. Long nights are inevitable sometimes."

Recker nodded, agreeing, and understanding his point. He wound up only sleeping about three hours himself. He was hoping that he'd be able to turn the tables on Jones and give him the information this time.

"Find out anything yet?"

"Indeed, I have," Jones said, turning around. "I've cross checked everything I've been able to get my hands on to verify what Mr. Ridley told you about them not having problems with anyone. As far as I can tell, that's completely accurate. He was also correct in that they've had no work done in their home that I can find."

"So that leaves us the nannies?"

"Meghan Carkner, twenty-four years old, college graduate in education from Temple."

"Any sketchy characters in her family tree?"

"None that I can find. Mom, dad, brother, none have ever had any brushes with the law, other than the odd speeding ticket," Jones turned back to his screen.

"How about a boyfriend?" Recker said, looking for an angle.

"Currently single. No exes that would seem to fit the profile."

"Why do I get the feeling you're saving the best for last?"

"Because I am." Jones smiled.

"Deanna Ambersome, twenty-eight years old. Before

she became a nanny for the Ridley's, she worked in retail and was fired from two different employers after she was found stealing merchandise."

"That would jive with what the Ridley's thought about her and why they fired her. That doesn't really prove anything, though," Recker said. "It's a long leap from stealing merchandise where you work to kidnapping somebody's child."

"Her family background would make her a more convincing candidate, however."

"What you got?"

"Mom's been in and out of jail several times for both drug possession and intent to sell. Dad's currently in prison for armed robbery."

"Sounds like a model family."

Jones put his hand up to continue. "Wait, it gets better. She currently has a boyfriend who's been in jail twice, once for assault and once for a home invasion."

"Home invasion? Small jump from that to kidnapping," Recker thought they might finally be on to something.

"There's also a brother. He's also been in jail once for burglary."

"The family that crimes together."

Recker sat on the edge of the desk and batted his eyes around the room, letting all the information that he just heard sink in. Jones swiveled his chair around to face his partner.

"What are your thoughts?" Jones wondered.

"I'd say we definitely have a couple of good suspects. The background is there."

"So, Deanna was upset at being shown the door and sought to get even somehow?"

"Sounds about right," Recker said.

A painful look took over Jones' face as he tried to understand the motivations. "Even if that's the case, why take a little girl? I mean, she has nothing to do with anything. Why do you put her in harm's way to get back at the parents, even if you feel they wronged you in some way?"

"You're trying to think like a normal, logical, caring person. These people aren't any of those things. Remember what I told you. Mara and Deanna didn't really hit it off, anyway. The child means nothing to her. She has no attachment to her. If they did this, she doesn't really care what happens to her at this point. It's just a means to make money and get back at the people who fired you," Recker said. "Can you work your magic to find out where all those people are at right now?"

Jones turned back to the computer and started pounding away on the keyboard again. "Working on it as we speak."

While Jones was busy trying to dig up their addresses, Recker went over to the gun cabinet. He opened it and examined his choices. He pulled out two pistols and an assault rifle, plus plenty of ammunition for each. He set them down on the desk as Jones continued to work his magic.

"Got it," Jones excitedly said.

"Where are they?"

"Looks like Deanna and her boyfriend are currently renting a three bedroom twin home in Frankford."

"I'll send the address to your phone," Jones said, looking at the weapons on the desk. "Do you really think you'll need all that?"

"Like I always say, I like to be prepared. If they're there, and Mara's there, they may not want to go away quietly. And I'm not leaving until I have that child," Recker replied.

"Should I accompany you as backup?"

Recker smiled at the notion, but didn't think Jones would be much help if a gunfight broke out. He'd probably be more of a liability than not, as it'd be one more person Recker would have to look after.

"You'll be better off here. Besides, if they're not there, that'll take you out of the game for a little while. You're of more use right where you're at. I can handle whatever's there." Recker smiled at him by way of encouragement.

Recker grabbed his guns, putting the pistols in their holsters, while putting the rifle in a bag to conceal it. He checked his phone on the way to the parking lot for directions. Ambersome and her boyfriend had a house rented on Bermuda Street. He drove a little faster than usual, wanting to get there as quickly as possible, just in case Mara was there and arrived just over twenty minutes later. He found the address and parked along the street a few houses down. He got out of his truck and hid the rifle inside his trench coat. He stood a few houses away from Ambersome's address, waiting to see if he noticed any activity in the building. It was a two story, brick lined building with a covered porch. There were two white chairs just in front of the window. It seemed to be a decent area, all the homes appeared well kept, no shuttered or abandoned houses that Recker could tell. He waited about ten minutes without seeing any movement from in or around the house. Assuming he wasn't likely to see anything else, Recker started walking toward the house. He got to the porch and put his left foot on the first step leading up to it, putting his right hand on the pistol inside his coat. He turned his head slightly, trying to hear anything from inside the house. He picked his head up when the door to the neighboring house swung open, a woman stepping onto her porch. Recker sized her up for a minute to make sure she wasn't a threat. She appeared to be in her fifties, and had a newspaper in her hand as she sat down on her rocker. The woman looked at the stranger stepping onto the neighbor's porch and wondered what he was up to. He looked like a cop, so she didn't say anything to him. Now fully on the porch, Recker stood next to the window out of sight, and carefully looked inside.

"Nobody's home," the neighbor finally said.

Recker looked over at her, then back inside the window again. Satisfied that he was leveling with her, he stopped looking through the window and walked over to the small metal fence that separated the two porches. "You know the people that live here?"

"Yeah. You a cop?" she asked.

"Do I look like one?"

"Yeah."

"Then there's your answer," Recker said.

"Which one you looking for?"

"Deanna and her boyfriend,"

"What do you want them for?"

"Routine investigation. Their names have come up as suspects in a case I'm working on and I need to talk to them."

"Good luck with that. They ain't been here in at least a couple of weeks," she said.

"Really? How many people have been living here?"

"Just Deanna and her boyfriend. Her brother comes around a lot too."

"You know where they might've gone?"

The woman shook her head, "no idea. Me and them weren't friends. I'm glad they haven't been around. Maybe their lease ran out, not sure."

"Why is that? They cause a lot of trouble?" Recker wondered.

"Nothing too bad. Just a lot of small stuff, you know? Music too loud, parties late at night, that sort of thing. Actually, now that I think about it..." She hesitated.

"What's that?"

"A few weeks ago, just before they disappeared, I heard them talking on the porch. I was inside, but they were talking loud enough for me to hear."

"What were they talking about?"

"I'm not sure. Seemed like a big disagreement at first, but the boyfriend smoothed it over."

"What were they saying?"

"Couldn't hear everything clearly, but the boyfriend

said something like, 'if we do this right and pull it off, we'll never have to worry about money again'. Sounded like they were gonna rob a bank or something."

"Well, I got a warrant here to search the house, so I'll be in there for a little while," Recker told her.

"They didn't really rob a bank, did they?" The woman looked worried.

"No. Something a lot worse."

Recker didn't say another word and kicked the door open. Before entering, he looked back at the neighbor and smiled.

"Aren't there supposed to be a lot more of you during these searches?" the woman said. "On TV, there's always like ten or fifteen guys looking through houses."

"We're a little shorthanded today," Recker said. "Couple of the guys called in sick."

Recker went inside and started turning the place inside out. It was already a little messy, a few dirty clothes on the floor and whatnot. He threw the cushions off the couches, looked through cabinets and closets, searched all the rooms, looking for any piece of evidence he could find that would indicate where the suspects had gone off to. He spent an hour in the home, going through each room several times, just in case he missed anything the previous time. Unfortunately, he wasn't able to find a single shred of evidence of where they were going. Not a piece of paper, not a receipt, no credit card statements, nothing at all. Recker sighed and shook his head, frustrated that he wasn't able to find anything. Standing in the middle of the living room, he let Jones know of his findings.

"Professor, just got done tossing the place," Recker said.

"And how did you fare?"

"Came up empty. They were either very careful, or just lucky, that they didn't leave anything behind."

"Or they didn't yet know where they were going," Jones said. It was a fair point.

"Kidnapping a child and asking for ransom isn't something you do on a whim. You need a plan. A good one. And it needs to be in place before everything unfolds."

"I'll start checking former addresses on my end. They didn't, by chance, leave any computers behind, did they?"

"No."

"Too bad. If they had, I could've searched through their history and possibly come up with their current location from there."

"No such luck," Recker said. "We'll have to do some more digging. What about cell phones?"

"I've already checked into that. It appears they've smartly gone with the prepaid variety. Even if they hadn't, the signals bounce off towers, I wouldn't be able to get an exact location anyway, just a general area."

"Better than anything we got right now. What about credit cards? Can you track them?"

"Yes, I could. But that would presume they had them and were using them."

"So they're not?"

"They have them, though they're currently over their spending limits," Jones said.

"So I take it that they're not using them."

"That would be correct."

"I don't suppose the boyfriend or brother have current jobs, do they?" Recker asked, not confident about the answer.

"They do not. At least, not of the legal variety."

"Man, we're really striking out here."

"Why don't you come back to the office and we'll figure out a plan from there?"

Recker did as Jones wished and went back to the office, where both of them worked the computers, shuffling back and forth between several computers at a time. Once they found the former addresses of Ambersome, her boyfriend, and her brother, Recker went to each location, hoping to turn up one of them. Since posing as a cop worked the first time, he played the part again, hoping it'd work just as well. He spent most of the day checking out the addresses, driving all over the city. Just like the first time, though, each one turned up nothing of value. Each house was occupied by either new tenants or homeowners, none of whom knew the current whereabouts of the people who lived there before they did. The cop routine worked again as well, somewhat surprisingly to Recker.

After exhausting the search of their former addresses, Recker and Jones spent the rest of the night in the office, still continuing their search. Once again, they worked right up until midnight. This time, neither one of them left to go home. They both took up residence on one of the couches to get a few hours of sleep. Recker woke up around five from the sound of the door closing. It was Jones with a couple of cups of coffee, fresh from the neighborhood convenience store. Recker sat up on the couch as Jones handed him his cup, taking a few minutes to fully wake up.

"What time'd you get up?" Recker asked.

"About four."

Recker shook his head. Jones had beaten him again. Jones sat down at the desk and started to work, still trying to find any connection to their suspects. A few minutes later, Recker joined him at the desk, taking one of the other computers. Throughout the entire morning, anytime they came up with a lead, even the smallest of leads, Recker went out to run it down. Each time was as frustrating as the time before. Ambersome and her cohorts didn't seem to be the type of criminals who'd excel at covering their tracks since it wasn't their usual type of crime, but they appeared to be doing a masterful job at it. Recker got back to the office at noon, and he wasn't in the greatest of spirits. Jones picked up on his mood as soon as he walked in and attempted to lift it. He called him over to the desk immediately to see what he picked up on.

"This just came in about five minutes ago," Jones said, playing an audio file. "It's from the device Mr. Ridley put on his phone."

"Have you got the money yet?" The same voice as before.

"I've only got some of it," Ridley said. "The rest is gonna take a couple more days."

"Your daughter doesn't have a couple more days!"

"Please, I'm trying to come up with it quickly. It takes time though. I don't just have that much money in the bank. It takes a couple of days to sell everything and get the money in my account."

"I don't wanna hear excuses. You have until five o'clock tomorrow night. If you don't have it by then, you might as well start making reservations for the cemetery, cause that's where your daughter will end up!"

"Please, no! I've done as you've asked. I haven't brought in cops or anything. Please, just don't hurt her."

"No more excuses."

Nothing but silence came after that. "Is that it?" Recker said.

"Yes." Jones smiled. "But it was enough for me to get a small trace on it."

"You got their location?" Recker said, surprised, hope in his voice.

"No. Not quite. It wasn't long enough for me to do that. I can tell that it's somewhere in the city though."

Recker slumped into a chair, dejected. "That really doesn't tell us anything then. We already knew that. We're not any closer to finding her than we were two days ago."

"Don't lose faith, Michael. Us getting frustrated won't help get Mara back," Jones said.

"I know. Time's running out, though. You able to turn up anything else?"

"Not so far."

Ten more minutes went by, Recker contemplating their options. He had an idea that might work. He'd need the cooperation of some unlikely people who might not be all that willing to help.

"If the Ridley's don't come up with that money by

tomorrow, what do you think will happen?" Jones said, thinking aloud.

"Depends on the kidnappers. If they're greedy and want all of it, they might be willing to wait an extra day or two for Ridley to get it. Or, if they're getting jumpy and just want to move on, they might just tell him to bring what he's got and be done with it. Or, there's a third option."

"Which is?"

"They could not bother with it anymore and cut bait," Recker said.

"You mean they could kill Mara?"

Recker nodded. "It's a possibility."

"We can't let that happen."

"Or there's another option," Recker said.

"Which is?"

"Even if Ridley doesn't have the money, we tell him to tell them that he does. Then when he makes the exchange, I take out whoever's there."

"That could be risky."

"Could be. They might not bring Mara to the exchange site in case they expect funny business. If she's at another location, and the cash doesn't show up, they might cut their losses and go."

"Which do you think would be the best way to go?"

"To find her before any of that takes place," Recker said.

"Then we'll have to bear down."

Then, Recker decided to blurt out what he was thinking. "There's one other thing we can try."

"What's that?"

"Remember what I told you before? All this computer stuff is great, but sometimes it doesn't beat intelligence on the street and having contacts."

"How does that come into play now?"

"I'll use the contacts I have to find her."

"Are you referring to Mr. Gibson and Jeremiah?" Jones said, a tone of disbelief in his voice.

"They know the streets. They might know something. That's not all. Tyrell also knows Vincent, he's a major player in the northeast. If they're in his territory, he might know something about it or where they're at."

"You're taking a very big leap of faith, don't you think?"

"No. Not a leap of faith. A leap of desperation," Recker said. "We're running out of leads and we're running out of time. So is Mara. I'm willing to do just about anything at this point to find out where she is. Even if that means conversing with the underworld."

"You actually think they'd be willing to help?"

Recker shrugged. "Only one way to know... ask."

11

Recker and Jones deliberated the merits of asking the gang leaders to assist in their search of Mara Ridley. They would almost certainly want something in return for their help, assuming they would be willing to begin with. If they did, they'd have to deal with that when the time came. Deanna Ambersome, her boyfriend, Derrick, and her brother, Marcus, had effectively disappeared. They had to utilize all available options that they had at their disposal. Recker took out his phone and called Gibson.

"Hey, need you to do me a favor," Recker said.

"What? You need a tank? A bazooka?" Gibson said sarcastically. "How about an F-15?"

"Could you get me one?"

"No, I can't get you a plane!"

"Never hurts to ask."

"So, whatcha want?" Gibson said.

"I need to meet with Jeremiah and Vincent,"

"At the same time?!" Gibson was shocked at the request.

"Doesn't have to be. Separate will work."

"What do you want them for?"

"Business."

"You're gonna have to do better than that, man. They're gonna ask me and I'm gonna have to tell them something. Me saying 'business' ain't gonna get it done," Gibson said. "They're not gonna meet unless they got a legit reason to."

"OK, fine. There's a little girl that's been kidnapped and being held for ransom. Her life may be in danger. The exchange is supposed to go down tomorrow at five. I'd like to get to them before that."

"So what exactly do you want them to do?"

"I just wanna know if they might have any intel on what's going on or if they've heard any rumblings. If they're the kings of their turf, maybe they know something."

"I'm not sure they're gonna give two hoots about some kid missing," Gibson said.

"She's an innocent four-year-old child, Tyrell. Imagine if that was your brother missing."

"All right, man, all right. I'll put the word out. I can't guarantee anything though."

"All you can do is try."

"What time you looking for?"

"As soon as possible," Recker said.

"All right. I'll get back to you if I hear anything."

Recker put his phone down on the desk and stared at the wall, thinking about his upcoming meetings with the two crime bosses. Though he didn't know how it'd turn out, he was fairly certain the two of them would at least meet with him and hear what he had to say. Jones finished up what he was doing on the laptop before inquiring about Recker's conversation.

"What did Mr. Gibson have to say?"

"He'll put the word out and get back to me if he hears something."

"What do you think?"

"They'll agree to meet," Recker said confidently.

"What makes you so sure?"

"Curiosity. Plus, I haven't met Vincent yet, and if he's heard about me, which I'm assuming he has, he'll want to finally meet face to face."

"You think they'll help?"

"Maybe."

"You may have to sweeten the pot for them," Jones said.

"We'll see."

An hour went by and Recker had just returned to the office with a couple of sandwiches for the two of them for lunch. They ate while they worked and quickly downed the turkey club. As the last bite of the sandwich went down Recker's throat, he took a sip of his soda to wash it down. His phone started ringing, and he wiped his hands off before answering.

"What's up, Tyrell?" Recker had his fingers crossed for good news.

"You owe me for this one, you know that right?"

"I'll make it good."

"All right, Jeremiah said he'll meet with you in an hour," Gibson said.

"Where at?"

"Same place as before. You remember it?"

"I'll be there. What about Vincent?"

"I'm still waiting to hear back from him. I'll let you know."

"Thanks."

Recker hung up and immediately informed Jones that the meeting with Jeremiah was all set. Though he wasn't yet sure exactly what he was going to say to him, Recker went through a couple of different scenarios in his mind. Both positive and negative ones. Though he was accustomed to high leverage situations, Recker was still a little anxious for the hour to pass. Most of the times when he was looking for someone, it was to kill them. This time was different. This time, it was to save a life. One that he had no personal connection to, but one that he felt a certain responsibility for. Even though the Ridley's didn't initially ask for his help, with his skills and his past history, he felt he should be able to handle these types of situations.

After a few minutes, Recker left the office to drive to the meeting. He wanted to get there a few minutes early, just in case there was traffic. He got to the house about five minutes early and saw the red bandana on the boarded-up window. He started walking up the concrete path toward the door when he noticed it opening slightly. A large man appeared in the doorway, waiting for him to arrive. Once he got there, the man put his arm out, directing Recker into the living room. There, Recker saw the same table and chairs they did business at before. He took a quick look around the room and noticed Gibson was absent. Surrounded by five of Jeremiah's men, scattered throughout the room, Jeremiah was seated at the end of the table, waiting for his visitor.

"So what do I owe this pleasure?" Jeremiah asked. "Tyrell said something about a missing kid."

Recker pulled a chair out and sat down across from him. "A four year old girl was kidnapped. I'm trying to find her and bring her home."

"What's in it for you? Why do you care?"

"Let's just say I have a rooting interest in it," Recker said.

"The family hire you to get her?"

"Uh, let's just say I'm working with them."

"So is that what you're doing here? Working for the highest bidder? Mercenary? Gun for hire?"

"I'm not for hire."

Jeremiah grinned at the seemingly always coy man across from him. "Tell me about this girl you're looking for."

"Parents live on Spruce Street. Suspects are Deanna Ambersome, Derrick Ianetta, and Marcus Ambersome. All have lengthy rap sheets."

"So you can't find them and you want my help?"

"That's pretty much the size of it," Recker said.

"What makes you think I know?"

Recker shrugged. "I don't. If you've done business with them, if you know of them, if you know what happened, I just thought maybe you'd heard something."

"What makes you think I care about some high rollers on the other side of town?" Jeremiah wondered.

"Because it's not about her parents, or you, or me," Recker said, stating his case. "The only thing it's about... is the life of a four-year-old child. That should go beyond anything. Race doesn't matter, wealth doesn't matter, location doesn't matter. The only thing that matters, is that the life of an innocent little girl is in danger. That should take precedence over anything. Now, I know you got your code that you live by, just like I've got mine. But when a child's life is in danger, any child, any bravado that we imply should go right out the window."

Jeremiah was silent as he let Recker speak his mind. He put his index finger on his mouth and rubbed his lip as he listened, not taking his eyes off the former military man. "You should've went into politics. That was a nice speech."

"Only difference is I meant every word."

Jeremiah glanced around the room as he thought about it. "Only problem is that I don't know them."

"It was worth a shot."

"I'll do one for you though," Jeremiah said. "I don't know these cats, but I'll have my boys put the word out on the streets."

"I'd appreciate that," Recker said.

Jeremiah nodded to one of his men to come over. "Start putting the word out to the boys and see if they know anything about a missing kid from Spruce. What were the names again?"

"Deanna and Marcus Ambersome, and Derrick Ianetta," Recker said.

"See if anyone knows them," Jeremiah told one of his soldiers. "If any of my boys know them or know where they're at, then I'll let you know."

"Good enough for me."

"I want something in return though."

Recker was starting to get up, but sat back down, anticipating a favor request might be coming. "What do you want?"

"Information."

"About what?"

"You," Jeremiah told him. "You played sly with me before about what you were doing here. I wanna know why you're here. You do that, I'll consider us even."

"There's only so much I can say."

"Tell me what you can."

"I've been hired by a private security firm to provide protection to certain individuals that they feel need it," Recker explained.

"Like this kid?"

Recker shrugged. "They tell me the assignment, I go do it."

"That's all there is to it?"

"That's it."

"So how do I contact this security firm? Maybe I'd like additional protection," Jeremiah said.

Recker smiled. "Not quite how it works. You don't hire them. They find their own clients."

"Or clients with criminal records?"

"That too." Recker grinned. "We good now?"

Jeremiah nodded. "Yeah. Yeah, we're good. For now."

Recker left the house and went back to his truck. He called Jones to let him know how the meeting went. After his conversation with the professor was over, he started driving back to the office. He'd only driven for a couple of minutes when his phone rang again. Stopped at a red light, he answered it.

"Tyrell?" he greeted. "Missed you at Jeremiah's."

"Yeah, well, I was busy setting other things up for you."

"Oh yeah?"

"Vincent agreed to meet with you," Gibson confirmed.

"Well that's good news."

"Yeah, well, we'll find out whether it's good or not when you're finished."

"Where and when?" Recker asked.

"There's a diner in the northeast in Mayfair called Pete's Place."

"Do all the diners in this city have first names?"

"What?"

"Nothing. What time?"

"They said now."

"I'm on my way."

"I'll give 'em the heads up," Gibson said.

Recker changed his course and drove the half hour to the diner. It wasn't a big place, and it didn't appear to be that busy since the parking lot was half empty. As Recker walked toward the entrance, it appeared that one of Vincent's men was standing guard at the door. If not, it'd be the first time he ever recalled a guard at the door of a diner. He certainly had the scowl of a mob henchman.

"You the man meeting Vincent?" the man asked.

"Maybe," said Recker.

The man put his hand out. "Need your iron."

Recker balked at the request and took a step back, ready for action if that's how the guy wanted to play it. "I don't hand my guns over to anybody."

"You'll get them back when you're finished."

Recker contemplated whether he wanted to comply with the request.

"Nobody sees the boss who's packing," the man said.

After a minute of deliberating, Recker thought it was best to agree. If time wasn't of the essence, and it wasn't regarding the life of a child, he might've just decided to take off. But now wasn't the time to balk and run. Recker reached inside his coat and handed his Sig over.

"And the other one," the man said, holding his hand out.

Recker grinned. "What makes you think there's another one?"

The man looked at him funny, like he thought he was some kind of sucker or something. "The other one."

Recker reached back into his coat and pulled out his Glock, handing it to the burly man.

"They'll be here when you come out." The guard held both guns in one hand.

As soon as Recker entered the diner, he was met by another man. This time it was Jimmy Malloy, Vincent's right-hand man and second in command. He didn't say a word to Recker, instead, just holding his arm out to guide Recker along. Malloy led him down to Vincent's table, a booth in the corner by the window. Vincent was about what Recker expected. He appeared to be in his mid-forties with short brown hair, and starting to go bald in front. Dressed in a suit, sans the tie, he looked the part of an organized crime leader. He was having a plate of spaghetti, soup on the side, as Recker sat down across from him. Vincent continued eating for a minute, looking at his companion as he did so.

Vincent wiped his mouth with a napkin before starting to talk. "So you're the man I've been hearing about," he said, smiling as if he just opened a present at Christmas.

"Could be."

"So you're Recker. I have the feeling you know more about me than I do of you."

"Possible."

"What's your first name?"

"Michael."

"Which nickname do you prefer? The man with the trench coat, trench coat man, or the latest one I read about, what was it... The Silencer?"

Recker smiled.

"I prefer The Silencer," Vincent said. "It's catchy, has a good ring to it." Vincent put his hand up and looked disgusted about something. "Where are my manners? Here I am eating in front of you and I didn't even offer you something. Would you like something? Soup, sandwich, some pasta?"

"I'm good. I've already eaten."

"Are you sure? They do serve a very good soup here."

"I'm fine."

"Sorry about having to take your guns, but it's for my own protection. I always do that when I'm meeting people I don't know for the first time."

"It's OK. I don't need them to kill," Recker said. "Just makes it easier and quicker."

Vincent grinned at his confidence and ate another forkful of his spaghetti before continuing. "So what brings you here to me?"

Recker cleared his throat before answering. "There's a four-year-old girl that was kidnapped a couple of days ago. I'm trying to find the people who took her before something bad happens."

Vincent nodded as he chewed his food. "Admirable of you. Why? What are the circumstances?"

"Kidnappers are looking for a million dollars by tomorrow at five o'clock."

"Do the parents have the capability of paying?"

"Not in the timeframe they're looking for," Recker said. "In any case, even if they can, I'm not sure they'll hand the girl over."

"So you think they might kill the girl either way?"

"I think it's possible. And I'd rather find them before we have the chance of finding out."

"Considering I haven't heard of this, I'm assuming the authorities have been left out of this arrangement?"

"Yes."

"I'm unclear what you think I can do for you," Vincent said, wiping his mouth with a napkin.

"I heard you were in charge of this territory. They might be in this area. They used to rent a house down in Frankford. Maybe you heard about it, or know where they might be."

"What makes you think I'm not involved in some way?"

"I don't know. I guess I just figured someone like you wouldn't stoop low enough to kidnap a child for ransom," Recker said.

"You're an intriguing man, Mike." Vincent fixed him with a stare. "You don't mind if I call you Mike, do you? What drives you to do this?"

"Do what?"

"This thing you're doing. Helping people. So far, I've read about you stopping rapists, murderers, robberies, even an arson."

"That's my job," Recker said as plainly as he could.

"How is it that you seem to keep appearing at that exact time of need when someone's in trouble?"

"Just seems to happen that way." Recker shrugged.

"I bet. You've got some type of inside information somehow that allows you to be there. Very ingenious."

"Luck more than anything."

Vincent shook his head. "No, I don't believe that. I don't believe luck has anything to do with it. You make your own luck in this business, or any other for that matter. People like to say it's luck, whether something good or bad happens, so they don't have to take responsibility for it. But it's anything but luck. It's the choices you make that put you in that position, in that very moment, when that supposed luck occurs."

Recker nodded, agreeing with his point of view.

"You work on your own? Have a team? Or a boss?"

"Well, you have your secrets, I have mine."

Vincent smiled. "So what is it exactly that you want me to do?"

"Put the word out and see if any of your men or contacts know where they are. I'm not looking for anything except information. If you find their location, let me know, I'll take care of the rest."

"Going to kill them?"

"Unless they decide to give themselves up, I imagine that's what it'll come down to," Recker assumed.

"Why do you think I'd even be willing to help you?" Vincent forked some spaghetti.

"After meeting you, you seem like an intelligent man, well dressed, like to eat well... what I can't figure out yet, is what you're willing to do to protect yourself."

"I'm not sure I understand your meaning."

"You like having money, power, having people look up to you and fearing you. I would think someone as smart as you would understand that things like this would bring heat on you. If that kid gets killed in your territory, that's gonna bring a lot of heat from the police in this area, not to mention the bigger media presence. If you like to operate in the background, that wouldn't exactly be good for business. Plus, if something like that goes down without your knowledge, people will start questioning whether you're actually in control. That wouldn't exactly be good for your little empire, especially since you're trying to expand your power base," Recker said.

"What makes you think I'm looking to expand my power? What makes you think I'm not content with what I have?"

"You hear things. People are never content with what they have. People who have a little bit of power always want more. Human nature."

Vincent smiled, a pleased look on his face as Recker seemed to accurately describe him. "So do you have names for these people that you're looking for?" he asked, picking up his glass of beer.

"Deanna Ambersome, Marcus Ambersome, her brother, and Derrick Ianetta."

Vincent finished taking a sip from his glass and was halfway to putting it down when he heard the names. His arm froze, recognizing the last of the names, looking at Recker before turning his eyes back on his glass. Recker noticed his hesitation upon hearing the names and knew he struck a nerve.

"You know them?" Recker asked.

Vincent looked at Malloy before answering. The pleasant look on his face slowly disappeared, replaced by a look of disgust. "I know Derrick Ianetta. He's done some work for me in the past."

"You know where he's at?"

Vincent threw his hands up, "he's more of a freelancer. He's not a permanent member of my organization. He's done a few jobs for me but nothing recently. Haven't heard from him in a few months or so."

"Deanna's his girlfriend."

Vincent motioned for Malloy, sitting at a nearby table,

to come over to them. "Derrick Ianetta. He kidnapped a child a few days ago and could be in the area," he said to him. "What were the others' names?"

"His girlfriend, Deanna Ambersome, and her brother, Marcus."

"Find them," Vincent said sternly.

"Yes, sir," Malloy said, leaving immediately.

"I guess I'll owe you a favor if you can find them," Recker said.

"We'll talk about that if we find them," Vincent told him. "Give me a number I can reach you in the event we do find them."

Recker grabbed one of the napkins on the table and wrote his number down on it. He slid it along the table in front of Vincent, who looked at it, then put it in his pocket. They concluded their business and Recker left the diner, making sure he picked his weapons up again from the guard at the door. He left in a better mood than he came in, sensing that they were now getting closer to finding Mara.

12

Though Recker and Jones continued their search for Mara, there really wasn't much more that they could do. They turned over all the leads that they could. Everything just came up empty. They didn't want to put all their faith in Jeremiah or Vincent, though, so they kept on plugging away. Mr. Ridley called Recker on the phone he gave him sometime during the night to ask about his progress, but Recker informed him that they hadn't found the kidnappers yet, though they were sure who was behind it. He did tell Ridley that they had a few more leads to track down and not to give up hope. The night passed, both of them sleeping in the office again. They woke up before the crack of dawn again. They passed on breakfast this time, neither having much of an appetite, knowing how high the stakes were about to become later in the day.

"I don't think I've ever rooted so hard for criminals to succeed in my life," Jones said.

Recker didn't respond to the comment, but agreed and understood the meaning behind it. A little after nine o'clock, Recker's phone rang, getting their hopes up before he saw who was calling. Hopes were quickly dashed when he saw it was Mia. Not that he was disappointed to talk to her, but he was hoping for news from one of the crime leaders.

"Hey," she said.

"Everything OK?"

"Yeah. Haven't seen or heard from you in a few days and I was thinking about you."

"Bored, huh?" he said.

Hendricks laughed. "No, nothing like that. I was just wondering if you wanted to get together for breakfast or something. I'm working the mid-shift today and just thought maybe we could get together."

"I'm sorry, I can't today. I'm not that hungry." Recker felt bad for turning her down.

"Oh." She sounded dejected. "Are you working a case?"

"Yeah." He kept it simple, not wanting to get into details.

"Maybe when it's finished then?" she said.

"Yeah, that sounds good."

"OK. I'll call you in a couple of days then?"

"Should be fine."

"OK. Talk to you then. Be careful."

"I will."

Once he saw Recker hanging up, Jones spoke up. "Are you sure it's wise to keep her involved?"

"She's not involved," Recker said.

"If she's close to you, then she's involved."

"I told you before, if something happens, it'd be good to have a nurse on our side to avoid a public hospital trip. She already knows about my past, we can trust her. Believe me, I have good instincts on who I can and can't trust."

Jones nodded. "I know. I guess I just don't want to see you get hurt again."

Recker smiled. "Professor, I didn't know you cared so much. I'm touched."

"Yes, well, let's see if we can get back to work and find Mara before it's too late."

They worked right up until noon, nothing new coming in. Recker went out to get them lunch since they were starving from missing breakfast. They got about halfway through when Recker's phone rang again. A look of hope dashed across Recker's face when he saw it was Tyrell. Maybe he had some good news for him.

"Tyrell, tell me you have something."

"Afraid not, man. Just talked to Jeremiah, and he wanted me to let you know that he came up with nothin'. He said his boys combed the streets but they have no idea where those bulls are."

Recker sighed. "I was afraid of that. Well, tell Jeremiah I said thanks for checking. I appreciate his help. You too, thanks for setting things up."

"Yeah, no sweat, man. Listen, I hope you find the girl. I really do."

"Yeah, me too," Recker said, and he meant it too.

By the sight of Recker's body language, Jones could

sense that he'd gotten a negative answer from his contact. He asked the question anyway, just to be sure.

"I take it that didn't go as well as we would've hoped?"

"Yeah," Recker said, a hint of despair in his voice.

"Well, we still have Vincent."

Recker nodded, not having anything else to say.

"What do we do if Vincent doesn't find them by five?" Jones had been dying to ask but didn't want to jinx things.

"Then I'll accompany Ridley to the meeting place and try to make sure that everything goes according to plan."

"And if it doesn't?"

"Then I'll have to improvise." Recker's face was set in a hard stare.

Two more hours went by, neither man saying another word as they worried about what was about to happen in another couple of hours. A little after two thirty, Recker just about jumped off his chair in excitement when he heard his phone ringing. Since it was a number he didn't recognize, he thought it had to be Vincent.

"Hello?" Recker answered it, hoping he was right.

"Michael, good to hear your voice again," Vincent said pleasantly.

"I hope you have good news for me."

"Well, I have news. Whether it's good or not, I'll leave up to your judgment."

"OK?"

"A couple of my men have found two of them," Vincent said.

"Great. Where?"

"They're hiding out in a house over in Mayfair."

"Which ones?"

"Derrick and Deanna. I'm not sure about the other one yet."

"Question them yet?"

"We're about to go in in a few minutes. I thought I'd give you the courtesy of joining us in the discussions if you'd like," Vincent said, giving him the address.

"I can be there in twenty minutes."

Recker hung up and rushed over to the gun cabinet, eagerly trying to get himself ready.

"I take it we have good news?" Jones said, watching Recker move faster than he'd ever seen.

"Vincent found Deanna and Derrick in a house over in Mayfair. He's about to go in and question them now. I'm gonna go meet them."

"What about the brother?"

"No word about him yet," Recker said. "I'll let you know what we come up with."

Recker rushed out the door and down the steps, running to his truck with his bag of guns in hand. He peeled out of the parking lot and raced down the highway, jumping on I-95 to get there quicker. Once Recker turned onto the street, he immediately noticed Vincent's guys. They were hard to miss. There were about ten of them gathered in front of one particular house. Recker parked his truck, then walked toward the house.

"You Recker?" One of the men challenged him as he approached.

"Yeah."

"Boss is inside waiting for you."

Recker walked past the men and noticed Malloy standing in the frame of the doorway.

"You got here fast." Malloy grinned.

"I'm on the clock."

Malloy led him into the living room. Vincent was circling around Deanna and Derrick, seemingly in a calm mood. The two suspects were sitting in a chair each, side by side, their hands tied behind the backs of the chair. By the looks of it, Vincent had already done his share of interrogating the pair, as both had cuts and bruises on their faces, spots of blood on each of them. Deanna had a cut on her forehead, while Derrick had a cut above his eye and blood running down the side of his face. Recker looked at Vincent's hand and didn't notice any cuts or abrasions on it, leaving him to believe he wasn't the one who worked the two over. He glanced down at Malloy's knuckles and noticed they were red and had traces of blood on them.

"Mike, nice to see you." Vincent fake greeted him like an unwelcome guest at a dinner party. "You're just in time. We were just about to get to where they were hiding the child."

"She's not here?" Recker said.

"No. We've already searched through the house. The child isn't here, nor is the third member of their little group."

"Please Mr. Vincent, we didn't mean nothin'. We were just lookin' for a quick, easy score," Ianetta interrupted.

"You disrespected me by bringing unwanted and unneeded attention by this little stunt of yours," Vincent responded. "If you wanted money, you should've come to me and I might've been able to give you a job or something. Instead, all you've done is bring down the heat."

"Where's the girl?" Recker said.

Ianetta spit in Recker's direction, sure that this man had something to do with his current predicament. Vincent looked to the ground, displeased at Ianetta's behavior. He gave a nod to Malloy to continue roughing up their guests. Malloy came over and gave Ianetta a backhand across the right side of his face, before nailing him with a right across on the other side of his face. Vincent grabbed his underling's arm to prevent any further damage at the moment and stepped forward, standing in front of the captured man.

"This man is my guest and he will be treated with dignity," Vincent said. "You will not disrespect him in my presence and be uncourteous."

Ianetta spit out some blood and a tooth and took a deep breath. "I'm sorry."

"Where's your brother, Deanna?" Vincent asked very politely.

She hesitated before answering, "I'm not sure."

Malloy looked to his boss before acting. Then he got the signal and backhanded her across the face, then came across the other side with the open side of his fist. After roughing her up, he took a step back to let Vincent continue talking.

"I'm not sure what you think you have to gain by this, but I assume you know that you're not leaving here until we get the information we want."

Deanna looked over at Ianetta, who nodded at her to

tell their captors whatever they wanted to know. Since Ianetta had done work for Vincent, and was familiar with him, he knew what he was capable of. The best they could hope for now was just to be able to leave the house with their lives intact.

"Promise me you won't kill him," Deanna said.

Vincent paced a few steps before turning back to answer her. "I give you my word. I will not lay a hand on him."

Even though he reassured them they wouldn't kill her brother, she still was hesitant about giving up his location.

"Tell him!" Ianetta yelled, knowing what would happen if they didn't.

"Marcus is with the girl in a house on Devereaux," Ambersome said through tears and gritted teeth.

"I'm assuming he's armed?" Recker asked.

"What do you think?"

"Address?"

"6249." She sighed, knowing she had lost.

"Is he alone?"

She clenched her jaw tighter, not wanting to say another word.

"The man asked you a question," Vincent added.

"Yes. He's alone." Ambersome only answered reluctantly when Malloy stepped forward again.

Vincent immediately looked at Recker. "You go get the girl. We'll stay here with them."

Recker looked at the two sitting in the chair, then back toward Vincent. He nodded his head, knowing the probable fate that loomed over the two prisoners. He raced out of the house and got in his truck, zooming down the road to get to Devereaux Street, which wasn't too far away. While he was on the way to get Mara, Vincent still paced around the room, as Malloy got in a few more shots at the faces of both Ambersome and Ianetta.

"Please stop," Ambersome mumbled, just able to get her mouth open.

"I give you my word, Mr. Vincent, I'll never do anything like this again." Ianetta was trembling, barely able to open his eyes, and at some stage had pissed his pants.

"You see, the problem is, examples sometimes need to be made to keep the masses in line," Vincent said, stirring their fears.

"No. No," Ianetta said.

"Sometimes you need to do things that you really don't want to do to show that you're still in control. That you still have a tight grasp on things." He noticed the stain on Ianetta's pants and put a gloved hand to his nose.

"You're still the boss."

"Deanna, I'd like to offer you my condolences." He turned to the woman.

"Why?"

"Losing a brother is not an easy thing to live with," Vincent said.

More tears started rolling down Ambersome's face. "You told me you wouldn't kill him."

"And I will keep that promise. I will not kill him. Neither will any of my associates. But my friend, the one that just left here, you see, I didn't offer the same promise in regards to him. I'm quite certain he will kill your brother."

"Nooo!" she yelled.

"The only decision I have to make now is whether you two will be joining him."

"No. No. You know I can help you, Mr. Vincent." Ianetta pleaded one last time for his life.

"I really don't think you can, Derrick. You've become a liability that I can't trust."

Without saying another word, he looked at Malloy, then left the room. He heard Ambersome crying as he left, her knowing what their fate was. Malloy moved around to the front of them to ask them a final question.

"You want to see it coming?" Malloy asked the pair.

"Whatever," Ianetta said. "Just hurry up and..."

Malloy interrupted his sentence and didn't wait for an answer, quickly pulling his gun up and putting a bullet in Ianetta's forehead before he even knew what was happening. He moved over to his girlfriend's chair, though she was too busy crying to respond. She was looking down, not wanting to see the final blow coming. Malloy gently put the gun to the side of her temple and squeezed the trigger. The force of the blast knocked her chair over and onto the floor. He motioned to the others to follow him outside to rejoin the boss. Vincent was waiting on the porch as the others came out, looking up at the sky.

"Something wrong, Boss?" Malloy asked.

"Nothing, Jimmy. Nothing at all. Beautiful day out, don't you think?"

Malloy grinned. "A little chilly, but not too bad a day."

Vincent nodded. "Yes, not a bad day at all."

Once Recker arrived at Devereaux Street, he parked a few houses down, quickly getting out of his truck. He went around the back of one of the neighboring houses, carefully going from house to house, hopping some fences and ducking behind some large obstacles, making sure he wasn't seen, until he got to the one Marcus Ambersome was in. He quietly maneuvered to the back door of the house. Recker wiggled the handle of the door to see if it was locked. After a minute, he was able to pick the lock and slowly opened the door, hoping it didn't creak and give him away. The door led into the basement on the raised home. Recker quietly walked inside and started searching the room. Mara wasn't there. Recker assumed she must've been upstairs in one of the bedrooms. He went over to the stairs, standing at the bottom and looking up to where they led, up to a closed door. He climbed them and stood on the top step, putting his ear to the door to see if he could hear any voices. He clenched his grip on his gun a little tighter as he heard footsteps coming closer. Someone was walking back and forth past the door, apparently mumbling to themselves. After a couple of minutes, Recker figured it must've been Ambersome. It seemed as though he was trying to call his sister and getting frustrated that he wasn't able to get through. Recker waited about ten minutes before making his move, just to make sure there were no other people in the house. Satisfied that Marcus was alone, since he heard no other voices or movements, Recker decided it was time to act. He waited a few more minutes until Ambersome paced by the door again and then he would strike. Once Ambersome walked by the door to the kitchen, Recker waited for him to come back. As soon as he heard him walk by, Recker threw open the door and hit Ambersome in the back of the head, knocking the kidnapper to the floor. In one motion, Ambersome hit the floor, rolled over, and reached for his gun, which was tucked inside the front of his pants.

"Don't do it!" Recker shouted, having the drop on him.

Ambersome didn't listen and tried to pull his gun out, giving Recker no choice in his response. Recker pulled the trigger on his Sig Sauer, firing two shots into Ambersome's chest. Ambersome immediately slumped down further on the floor, the life evaporating from his body. Recker walked over to Ambersome's body and kicked his gun away from him. The bedrooms were upstairs and Recker ran up them to check for Mara. The first bedroom he checked was on the right. He opened the door and there she was. Just sitting on the floor in the corner with her knees up to her chest. Recker smiled at her and put his gun away. He walked into the room, trying not to frighten her any more than he knew she already was.

"Mara, my name's Michael," he softly told her. "I'm here to take you back to your mommy and daddy."

"Where are they?"

"They're waiting for you at home. I'm gonna take you there."

"Are you sure?" The little girl sounded understandably wary.

"Positive," he smiled. "Maybe if you're good, we can stop for an ice cream or milkshake on the way."

"Chocolate?" Mara asked, perking up.

"Whatever you want."

"OK."

"I'm gonna pick you up, OK? There's something down-stairs that I don't want you to see."

"OK."

Recker picked her up and went downstairs, shielding her eyes so she didn't see the dead body on the floor. He carried her all the way to his truck, putting her in the front seat. He didn't have a car seat for her, so at least by having her next to him, he could keep his eyes on her and talk to her. Before starting the car, he called Mr. Ridley and let him know that he had Mara safe and sound. He put Mara on the phone with him so her mother and father could hear her voice again and know she was all right. After a couple minutes, Mara handed the phone back.

"I promised Mara I'd stop on the way for a chocolate milkshake," Recker said. "Other than that, we'll be right there."

"I don't know how to thank you," Mr. Ridley said through gentle sobs in the background.

"There's no need."

Recker did as he promised and stopped to get Mara a chocolate milkshake, the biggest one they had. After that, he drove right to Spruce Street, the Ridley's waiting on the steps leading up to their front door. Recker pulled up right in front of their house into an empty spot. The Ridley's eagerly rushed over to the truck to see their daughter. Recker unlocked the door so they could open it. Her parents pulled her out of the truck and hugged her. Recker got out and walked around to the front of the truck and watched them, relieved that it was a happy ending. Mr. Ridley pulled himself away from his family to approach Recker.

"I don't know what to say."

"Nothing needs to be said," Recker said.

"While we were waiting, my wife and I were talking, we wanted you to have some kind of reward."

Recker put his hand out to prevent him from going any further. "I don't need any reward. Getting her home back to you safe and sound is reward enough."

With tears in his eyes, Ridley smiled and nodded. "You know, I never did get your name."

"It's not important. Your family's waiting for you," Recker told him, nodding in their direction.

With his work done, Recker drove back to the office. On the way, he called Vincent, just to let him know how it all turned out and to thank him for his help. It was a brief conversation as Vincent said he had other business to attend to, but he was glad to help. Once Recker got back to the office, Jones was waiting for him. It was the happiest Recker had seen him look since they started their little partnership together.

"I think I might wanna take tomorrow off," Recker said.

"You really think you've earned it?" Jones just couldn't resist a little lightweight needling.

Recker laughed, knowing he was kidding.

"By all means, Mike. You've earned the day."

"I think that's the first time you've called me that," Recker said.

"Then when you get back, we have more victims that will need our assistance."

"All in a day's work, right Professor? All in a day's work."

ABOUT THE AUTHOR

Mike Ryan lives in Pennsylvania with his wife, and four children. He is the author of the bestselling Silencer Series, as well as numerous other books. Visit his website at www.mikeryanbooks.com to find out more about his work, and sign up for his newsletter to be notified of new releases.

 facebook.com/mikeryanauthor
 instagram.com/mikeryanauthor

ALSO BY MIKE RYAN

The Eliminator Series

The Extractor Series

The Cain Series

The Ghost Series

The Brandon Hall Series

A Dangerous Man

The Last Job

The Crew